WRAPPED
WITH
Love

BETH BOLDEN

Author Note

In 2017 when I wrote *Wrapped with Love,* Harry Potter occupied an incredibly indelible place in our imaginations. I would argue that nothing has changed about how we as a culture and a people feel about the boy who lived in a cupboard under the stairs. However, since 2017, we've learned a lot about the author, JK Rowling, and her beliefs about trans rights, queer rights and human rights.

I want everyone reading this book to know that I unequivocally support trans rights, and queer rights (and of course, human rights!).

If you would like to learn more about how to support trans rights please visit the National Center for Transgender Equality.

PROLOGUE

"Chef, I think we have a problem."

Reed Ryan looked up from the garnishes he was impeccably arranging with steady, sure fingers on the plate in front of him. "What?" he asked calmly. Like so many other chefs who owned their own restaurants and were answerable only to themselves, Reed was a perfectionist. Unlike so many, he wasn't a particularly loud, angry or obnoxious one. He didn't yell. He didn't threaten. He simply expected all his employees' very best and if they didn't deliver, he'd ask for their apron at the end of service. No second chances.

"There's a man here who wants a table, but we're full." Danielle, who dealt with the front of the house, wrung her hands.

Reed barely spared her a glance. "This doesn't sound like an actual problem," he pointed out. "Tell them we're full, and that reservations are generally recommended on Saturday nights."

She hesitated. "It's not just anyone. It's Jordan Christensen."

"Who?"

Reed knew in a distant corner of his brain that he wasn't giving Danielle his full attention or even half his attention. At Garnet, the focus wasn't on the trendy décor or the killer happy hour that would bring in singles looking for their newest one-night stand. The focus remained solely–*exclusively*–on the food.

Not on the latest celebrity athlete who thought he was too good to make a reservation at one of Chicago's hottest destinations on a Saturday night.

"You know who Jordan Christensen is." Reed hadn't expected Danielle to call his bluff, but now that she had, he wasn't sure what to do about it.

"He's a man like every other man, right?"

Reed ignored how he'd looked last Sunday afternoon, spiking a football over the goal posts after a touchdown pass, his body elongated and the tight uniform emphasizing just how long and lean he was. He told himself it was easy enough to forget about it; all one required was the appropriate focus.

He took the bowl of delicately dressed microgreens and settled them in a lacy cloud on top of the venison steak. "Service!" he called and the plate was whisked away instantly.

Perfection.

Reed expected it, and Reed usually got it.

But Danielle was still standing there expectantly, waiting for Reed to take care of an issue that was above her paygrade.

Reed rolled his shoulders, trying to let out some of the unbearable tightness he suffered from after bending over plate after plate, hour after hour, night after night, making sure that every dish that passed through his hands was flawless.

The decision was a quick one. He wiped his hands on a towel and turned to Danielle. "Give them the private dining room. No menus. Chef's choice tonight."

Reed could tell it wasn't what Danielle had hoped for–she'd hoped that Reed would make a rare appearance on the dining side of the restaurant and send Jordan packing himself. But it wasn't in Reed's nature to turn people away, even arrogant bastards like Jordan Christensen.

Turning towards the stove, the sous-chef and line cooks parted respectfully as Reed approached. He looked up and down the line, focus razor sharp. "Private party. The lobster medallions. The clam pasta. And the wild mushroom bisque and the sweetbread salad to start. I want to see everything before it goes out. I'll make the sweetbreads myself."

It was a delicious menu, because everything that Reed created was, but it included some of the more unique, delicate dishes Garnet served. Reed was sure, as his hands turned into a whirlwind of precise, economical movements, that the football player and the rest of his party had come to Garnet expecting the wild game they were known for. The venison steak. The elk flank. Something hearty and protein-packed.

Something manly.

They were going to be surprised, and Reed was looking forward to it.

Reed's plan went wrong almost immediately.

He'd been absolutely certain that the menu, ambitious and almost certainly distinctly different from the private party's expectations, would defeat them.

Instead, Dan, who was waiting on Jordan's table, reported that the bowls and plates were empty, even the sweetbread salad. Even after Dan had been asked and explained exactly what they were eating. There'd been appreciation and surprise, but not, as Reed had anticipated, an ounce of disgust.

As a general rule, Reed was not easily impressed. He reasoned as he delicately twirled the pasta into the center of the plate with a pair of tongs that his expectations had started so low that Jordan and his friends couldn't help but exceed them.

When Dan came by the pass-through, a smug look on his face, Reed felt the slow burn of frustrated anger simmering in a hard knot inside his chest. He was going to have to work twice as hard at the gym tonight loosening it to fall asleep.

"They liked the clam pasta?"

Dan crossed his arms over his chest. All the servers Reed hired came to love the food. Reed knew Dan loved the clam pasta, but it was not something he'd ever expected some testosterone-laden gym rat who used his head as a battering ram would enjoy.

"They loved it."

Reed glanced over at the line, where he saw the lobster medallions being prepared.

He never shoved. He never yelled. But he definitely exerted some of the physical strength he'd gained from all those late-night workouts and his voice might have been a *tiny* bit louder as he stalked to the stove and began preparing the medallions himself.

They would be transcendent. They would be esoteric. They would be sublime. Jordan Christensen would admit he'd made a mistake by waltzing in here, expecting to be served.

"Service," Reed called as he gave one final glance over the four plates of lobster medallions. They looked just as delicious as they always did, and Reed, who'd taught himself to never doubt, felt an unusual concern that maybe he could have done something different to make them *better*.

Dan appeared as quickly as Reed wanted. Almost too quickly, he realized as Dan whisked the plates away. Maybe there could have been a molecule of sauce better placed. More seasoning? Less? Logically, he knew he'd done the best with his not-inconsiderable skill. There was nothing left to do but focus on the other plates for the other, equally as important, diners who had come to Garnet tonight.

But after the exquisite frustration of Jordan's dinner, everything felt flat and tense, and after ten minutes at the pass-through, even Reed could admit he needed a break.

He'd given up smoking in culinary school when he'd discovered quickly that both his palate and his body would need all the help they could get to make it through such unexpectedly grueling work. Serious cooking wasn't for anyone who wanted to take a shortcut, and it wasn't for anyone willing to compromise even an iota.

Instead, he leaned back on the brick wall in the alley next to the restaurant and breathed in the dark night air. Empty of distractions, his mind returned, predictably, to the game he'd watched last Sunday.

He didn't always watch football on Sundays, but after his morning run, he'd turned the game on, mostly on a whim. He'd ignored the annoying voice that informed him that since Jordan joining the Bears two years ago, Reed had watched significantly more football. He never let himself *plan* to watch it, but he still found himself catching more games than he missed.

Logically, Jordan Christensen was an attractive man, and Reed was in the middle of a dry spell that felt like a thousand years long because he couldn't ever relax enough to date anyone. It made sense that Reed would like watching him.

That was all.

And now Jordan was at *his* restaurant. Reed tipped his head back and wished that he could see the stars, but they were in downtown Chicago and the light pollution was terrible, making it impossible to even catch a glimpse in the night sky.

Maybe if he could see them, he'd feel less like he was going to explode out of his skin.

"Chef?"

Reed's head automatically whipped towards the open doorway. Dan's head was poking out of it, and he looked surprised, breaking the monotony of the "I'm a cool waiter at a trendy restaurant" façade that he was so good at.

Reed thought the astonishment made him look more human and less like a hipster robot.

"What is it?" Reed asked, trying to keep his voice calm and level. He felt like he'd been dipped in hot fat and was about to start sizzling.

"Jordan Christensen's private party asked if they could have a word with you."

It was definitely not unheard of to have high-profile visitors ask to speak to the chef. It wasn't even unusual for *non*-high profile visitors to ask to speak to Reed. But Reed, who knew how awkward he was in social situations, typically avoided it.

He should avoid it now. His head was too full of stray thoughts. He wasn't focused at all and it was a recipe for disaster, but Reed still found himself agreeing and following Dan into the restaurant, through the kitchen doors, and onto the dining room floor.

He was so much more comfortable in the kitchen, where he was in charge of everything he surveyed, instead of being gawked at like some sort of extinct creature. *A chef outside his normal habitat.*

Dan led the way into the private dining room, which was separated by a living wall garden.

Reed swirled the edges of his aloof chef persona around him like a bulletproof cloak, hiding away all those raggedy edges of social awkwardness and anxiety that he never wanted anybody to see. Especially the man in front of him.

He was vaguely aware that Dan was introducing him to the various people at the table. There was a woman there and she was with a man who must be another football player, and there was another guy in a snazzy suit, with a watch that probably cost a fortune sparkling on his wrist.

But all Reed had eyes for was Jordan.

He was even better-looking here, in the dim light of the restaurant, with the wall trailing greenery behind him, emphasizing the bright clarity of his eyes. He was even dressed well, a pair of slacks and a leaf-green polo shirt that almost, but-not-quite, matched those incredible eyes. No gym shorts or t-shirts. Reed was dangerously aware of his own stained chef's jacket that pulled across the muscles of his chest. Danielle was always telling him he needed to focus more on his appearance, to improve Garnet's marketability, but Reed had never regretted ignoring her until those green eyes gave a leisurely perusal of his person, top to bottom, then bottom to top.

"Jordan Christensen," the man in front of him said, standing and offering his hand.

Reed knew he could be shy, sometimes painfully so, and unfortunately that was never more in evidence than when confronted with a man he found desperately attractive.

Hot, Reed floundered, *he's* hot. *That's what Danielle would say.*

"Reed Ryan," he said, ignoring the flare of heat at the way the other man's strong hand closed over his, even for the briefest moment.

"Thank you for accommodating us tonight," Jordan said. "It was an . . . experience."

"A very special one," the woman said, chiming in. "I've never eaten sweetbreads before."

But Reed could only look at Jordan. That much was probably painfully obvious, but he still couldn't tear his gaze away.

"Next time," Reed said, his voice coming out in horrifically clipped tones that he didn't even recognize, "when you feel like sweetbreads, try to make a reservation."

Reed could hear Dan's astonished cough behind him. He could see the flash of surprise in Jordan's eyes. The woman's mouth falling open a little in shock. His own uneasy flight back through the dining room to the refuge the kitchen always provided him.

Later, he would try to convince himself that he hadn't meant to be an insulting ass. He wasn't sure he believed it, even after listing out all the reasons his behavior had made sense.

You wanted to prove he wasn't anything special.

You wanted to educate him.

You wanted to make him notice you.

You wanted to show him you were just as special as he was. Even if he is a football player and you're just a chef.

He definitely didn't believe it.

Instead, he went to the gym and worked his arms until they were burning. Did enough squats he wasn't sure he'd be able to stand the next day. Tried to exhaust himself until he couldn't see Jordan Christensen's shaken expression.

It didn't work.

"Chef," Danielle said patiently, following his dictated procedure perfectly. Get his attention, and then wait quietly until he'd finished what he was working on.

"What is it?" he asked. Trying to be his usual quiet, focused self. Trying to dampen the testy edge of his voice that he'd had so much trouble erasing lately.

It had been nearly a month since the Jordan Christensen debacle, and he was still having trouble looking anyone who knew about it in the eyes. He'd even considered finding Dan another job because it was so hard to continue working with him after he'd witnessed Reed's meltdown. But Dan was too good, and Reed knew he couldn't lose him over a little embarrassment, even if the incident still made him inwardly cringe.

"It's the reservation list for tonight," Danielle said, nervously tucking a strand of hair behind her ear.

It was a Wednesday night. It was possible to get into Garnet on a Wednesday without a reservation, so that in of itself wasn't unusual. It was the way Danielle couldn't meet his eyes. The same way he usually couldn't meet hers.

"It's Jordan Christensen," she finally broke down. "He's made a reservation."

Reed prided himself on remaining outwardly calm. He'd been through the hellfires of so many chaotic kitchens, he'd learned to project an appearance that he sometimes didn't feel.

He sure as fuck didn't feel calm right now.

"Oh?" he managed.

"It's for one," Danielle said. "Isn't that odd?"

It wasn't odd, though it might seem that way for a normal person. Lots of foodies traveled to his shrine alone. But Jordan? That did strike Reed as unusual.

"Maybe he likes eating alone," Reed suggested. "Lots of people don't like to be distracted from the food by conversation."

Danielle shrugged and shot him a look that spoke volumes. *Only you do that, you crazy person. You're just making excuses for being alone and not having anyone to go to dinner with you. Nobody* prefers *to eat alone.*

Or maybe that was his own devil's advocate. It was hard to say. Except it really wasn't.

This time, Reed let Jordan order from the menu because he was interested in seeing what the other man would choose on his own, but Reed still insisted on preparing every dish himself. Told his uncooperative, unfocused brain about a hundred times that the only reason Jordan would come back here after being treated so rudely was that he'd become addicted to the food.

Lots of people claimed that, and Reed had always felt a soft, amorphous affection for the obsessed. With Jordan, Reed *craved* his addiction. Hoped that the food he prepared for him tonight would solidify Jordan's desire for Reed's creations.

The first item Jordan ordered was the only repeat–the sweet-bread salad. Looking at the ticket sent Reed into a cold sweat even in the burning heat of the kitchen. Was it an apology? A pointed message? A *fuck you*?

Reed stewed over the possible meanings as he pan-fried the sweetbreads, nestling them in the plate of field greens, pepitas and sweet corn tucked in between the leaves like little jewels. Whatever Jordan had meant when he'd ordered this dish, Reed was going to make certain it was as flawless as he could prepare it.

Luckily, he didn't have an eternity to obsess over the dish. Mike, his sous-chef, grabbed it from his hands, slid it across the pass-through and then it was gone.

Reed couldn't remember the last time he'd glared at anyone in this kitchen, but he shot Mike a questionable look, even though they'd worked together for seven years.

"What?" Mike shrugged, though Reed had a strong feeling he knew exactly what was happening. "The sweetbreads need to be served piping hot. Contrasts with the fresh herbaciousness of the greens. Or at least that's what you've always told me."

"It's true," Reed said stiffly, awkward that he'd been so obvious. Obsessing over a diner. Obsessing over *Jordan Christensen*.

He and probably about a million other people in Chicago, most of them probably a gender that Jordan was actually interested in.

Reed had never let himself wonder if Jordan liked men. He'd written it off as an impossibility and closed the door behind the thought. It had seemed infinitely safer, even though he'd also come to the conclusion that meeting him was a slim possibility.

Turning back to the stove, Reed grasped for the tattered remnants of his focus and buckled down to help prepare the next wave of dishes as Mike called them out.

Still, every venison steak that Reed prepared, he hoped it was for Jordan.

When his dessert order came in, the lavender honey crème brûlée, Reed insisted on fetching it himself, carefully arranging it on the napkin and plate.

"Looks good, Chef," Dan said, and Reed barely refrained from glaring, even though the man's voice sounded perfectly neutral. One of the things he'd had to learn—and it had been a long, hard road—was that not everyone was laughing at him. Sometimes people said what they meant and there was no ulterior motive lurking underneath their words.

Dan was probably being honest.

Dan probably wasn't secretly laughing at his boss, who had never before been tempted to slip a piece of paper with his phone number underneath a dessert.

That still didn't stop Reed from pulling up the credit card slip from Jordan's check much later that night, after everyone had left and he was alone in his office, checking the sales from the dinner service.

At a bigger restaurant, he'd have a manager to do the accounting for him, but Reed liked that Garnet was small and liked that he still had his fingers in all its pies. And it also meant that he could check Jordan's credit card slip now without a single person being the wiser.

Unfortunately, all it told Reed was that the man was a generous tipper. No doubt Dan was thrilled at his luck. Reed leaned back in his office chair and groaned in frustration.

His trip to the gym tonight was going to need to be more brutal than ever. He needed to hit his bed and forget all about Jordan and his stupid green eyes.

Life would be so much easier that way.

Except Jordan came back the next week. Also on a Wednesday night, but this time, later in the dinner service. Danielle appeared in the kitchen halfway through, an apprehensive look on her face that told Reed everything.

He listened greedily as she told him that Jordan had called in, and had asked for one of the last tables of the night.

Normally, Danielle wouldn't keep Reed so intimately appraised of reservation details, but she'd clearly discerned that Jordan was an unusual case and that her boss wanted to be kept in the loop when it came to him.

Reed didn't want to think about how transparent he probably was, or the likelihood that his entire staff was amused by his unlikely crush.

He hadn't ducked out on a dinner service in eight months, but he seriously considered doing it tonight.

Garnet ran like a well-oiled machine, even in his absence. He could leave and Jordan would probably never know the difference in the quality of food that came from the kitchen. He'd never realize that Reed Ryan was a huge chickenshit.

He'd only realize if he asked for Reed and was told he wasn't there. Suddenly, Reed wasn't prepared for that eventuality.

"Let me know when he gets here," was all he said to Danielle.

In the hour and a half until the reservation, Reed checked his watch more than he had in the previous twelve hours. That wasn't an entirely scientific calculation, but from the way Mike smiled when he noticed, it was probably accurate.

Like the previous two meals that Jordan had at Garnet, he ended up seated in Dan's section. Reed wasn't sure that was on purpose or not, and made a note to ask Danielle if she'd seated him there or if he'd requested it.

Dan walked in and instead of posting an order on the pass-through, stopped and waited for Reed to finish plating a venison steak.

"Jordan is here. He'd like the chef's choice tonight."

Nobody else showed up at Garnet and had the nerve to request Reed decide what they were eating for dinner. If anyone else had asked, Reed would have rolled his eyes and refused to participate. When Jordan asked, every bit of Reed that had ever craved a cute boy's attention rolled over and started panting.

The fluttering at the base of his stomach lasted for a moment, and then Reed pushed it aside. He couldn't waste precious minutes when he could be deciding what to feed Jordan.

The sweetbread salad, of course, but altered slightly. He added some fresh roasted beets, goat cheese, and sprinkled with some candied pecans. It altered the salad from really good to fucking phenomenal. Reed decided to make it next week's special.

After serving the salad, Dan swung by the kitchen as Reed was agonizing over what to serve as a main course. The lobster and corn pot pie? The elk flank steak? He could repeat again with the venison steak and maybe snazz it up with a different side.

"Chef," Dan said, raising his voice so he'd be heard across the kitchen. Mike was at the pass-through because Reed had his hands full trying to feed his new favorite customer, though he'd told his sous-chef that with the dinner service coming to a close, he'd wanted to experiment with a new recipe. It was bad enough that Danielle knew about Reed's partiality to a certain NFL player.

"Yes?" Reed said, wiping his hands on a towel. He was about 80 percent mentally occupied trying to decide on a main course still—he'd pared the choices down to the lobster and corn pot pie and the elk flank steak—and he realized a half-second too late what Dan was about to say in full hearing of the entire kitchen.

Basically, if his little crush had been a secret before now, it was shortly about to become public knowledge.

"Jordan loved the changes to the sweetbread salad," Dan said, louder than Reed thought was entirely necessary. "He wanted you to know he's never liked beets before, either."

Mike chuckled. "Maybe he just likes Chef's beets."

Yeah, definitely not a secret any longer. *Shit.*

"Enough," Reed hissed with more annoyance than he actually felt. The good news was that the low-level buzz of whispered gossip flatlined to nothing, but he wasn't stupid enough to think that this wouldn't be hot news tomorrow. If he was unlucky, the talk would filter right through the culinary community of Chicago.

Reed Ryan has a thing for the Bears' favorite receiver.

He could only pray that Jordan wouldn't hear about it and never come back. After all, Jordan liking Reed's food didn't mean that he liked *Reed*.

"What's the main course?" Dan asked.

"Lobster and corn pot pie." Once he'd made a decision, Reed immediately knew it was the right one. That was why he'd replaced the corn in the sweetbread salad with the beets, wasn't it? He wanted to highlight the beautiful sweet corn they'd just gotten in from one of his favorite farms outside Chicago. He'd fold it into a thick but delicate thyme cream sauce, studded with lobster, and top it with the lightest, flakiest pie crust.

Jordan wouldn't know what hit him.

The beauty of dinner service was that even when faced with preparing a meal for Jordan, the distractions still all fell away. He was too focused making sure that the dish was as perfect as he could make it to agonize over the fact this was for Jordan.

When he placed the pot pie on the plate, with a single sprig of thyme as a garnish, the crust shone burnished gold under the heat lamp.

Reed wasn't stupid enough to think that a pot pie could create love, but he couldn't silence that tiny hopeful voice in his heart. He didn't even know if Jordan liked men, but that didn't matter anymore. Reed was all burning courage and anticipation as Dan took the dish to the dining room.

He was in his office, uselessly pushing paperwork across his desk when Dan appeared in the doorway.

"Jordan is asking for you, Chef."

There was a wealth of insinuation in Dan's words, but Reed brushed them aside. "He is?"

"Yes, he's ordered dessert for both of you, and he'd like you to join him."

Reed's eyebrows hit the edge of his hairline. The hope burned hotter. A request like this was unheard of–and Jordan had ordered dessert. For both of them. It was almost, sort of, a date.

"Tell him I'll be right there," Reed said before he could revert to his normal stupidity and say no.

As soon as Dan disappeared, Reed ducked into the kitchen bath-room and shed his chef's coat, hoping that the simple white t-shirt he wore under it wouldn't be too casual. He sniffed himself, and was relieved that even after five hours of dinner service, he didn't smell too awful. There wasn't anything to do about his buzzcut, or his straightforward features. He was who he was.

That was what he told himself as he walked into the dining room to try to calm his racing heart, but it didn't work.

Jordan was leaning back in his chair, the smug smile on his face evidence of a well-fed man. He was toying with the stem of a half-full wineglass in one hand, and was resting the other on the white tablecloth.

"Chef," Jordan said respectfully, sitting up in his chair as Reed approached.

Reed might be out of practice at dating, but he could still sense an ambush. Jordan had called for a reservation near the end of the dinner service. He'd picked a table in a section that would empty out first. And he'd taken his time eating.

Which all meant that they were essentially alone, if you didn't count all of Reed's employees, who were no doubt hovering as close as they could, desperate to hear something juicy.

Reed decided he didn't care.

"Call me Reed," he said as he sat down opposite Jordan. Sitting they were almost the same height. Standing, Reed thought Jordan would have more than a few inches on him. He'd have to tilt his head back to kiss him. His uncooperative heart thudded harder in his chest.

"Reed," Jordan said, and Reed knew he wanted to hear him say his name a thousand different ways.

He'd told himself no matter how terrible his nerves were, he would get this out of the way first, so he spoke before Jordan could. "First off, I need to apologize for my words the first time we met."

Jordan looked surprised. "You do?"

Reed ordered himself not to blush, but he did anyway. "I shouldn't have made the comment about the reservation. I was happy to serve you and your friends."

"But we should have had a reservation, right?" Jordan seemed unconcerned.

"It wasn't an issue, I promise."

Jordan smiled. "You wouldn't have said it if it wasn't. Which is why I should be the one apologizing. My agent is a conceited ass, and thought it would impress me if he could walk in and demand a table at Garnet."

The hope was a fiery conflagration now. "Did it?"

Jordan leaned forward, his eyes laser focused on Reed, contradicting his relaxed posture. "He knew what a big fan I am of yours. So yes. It did. Very much."

Reed's mouth was the Sahara desert. When would Dan get here with the dessert so he could ask for water? He was going to burn up before they even kissed for the first time.

And despite his usually terrible intuition about these things, Reed was becoming increasingly certain that they would.

CHAPTER ONE

TWO YEARS LATER

Reed stood in the entrance to the cute little roadside taqueria that overlooked the Pacific Ocean, sparkling in the late afternoon sunlight, and mentally tortured his ex-boyfriend with every kitchen implement he'd ever owned.

It felt as if the last sixteen terrible months had been a figment of his shitty imagination.

Jordan looked exactly the same. Still too tall. Still lean. Still all legs. Still with those green eyes that had always made Reed's heart skip in his chest whenever they'd turned his way. Still with that unfairly charming smile that had owned Reed from the first second they'd met, even when Reed had disliked him.

Fate, Reed thought sourly with a painful pang in the vicinity of his traitorous heart, *was a real bitch.*

Today, fate went by the name Nick Wheeler, and he just happened to be Reed's brand-new boss.

"I think you know Jordan Christensen," Nick said casually, like his words weren't bombs in Reed's brain. His heart. His even more traitorous dick.

Reed gave a slow nod–what else could he say? *Yeah, he's my ex. You know that ex you never get over? The one you still dream about? The one you hate and love in equal measure? Yeah,* that *ex. That's Jordan Christensen.*

"He hangs with us sometimes," Nick said. "I hope that'll be okay."

Another nod was all Reed could manage. It wasn't even a little okay, but it was also Reed's first day at *Five Points*, and he wasn't about to tell Nick that he would rather fling himself off this cliff than spend time with the man who had crushed, pulverized and then driven back and forth over his heart a few times for good measure.

Following Nick, Reed dragged his uncooperative feet towards the table where Jordan sat with a few other people.

Reed knew the exact moment Jordan registered just exactly who was approaching their table. His back stiffened, and anybody else might not have noticed, but Reed had spent the best (and worst) year of his life memorizing everything about Jordan, filing every detail away in his brain. It had made living without Jordan easy and impossible at the same time. He'd been able to recall every facial expression, every emotion in his eyes, the flex of every muscle, but they were only memories. Ultimately empty and meaningless without the real man in front of him.

"Reed!" a voice exclaimed from the other end of the table. Reed's gaze flickered up from Jordan, who *didn't* look all that surprised to see him, to the rest of the group.

"You remember Landon and Quentin, I'm assuming," Nick said smoothly from behind Reed. "To refresh your memory, Landon is the loud one."

Reed cleared sixteen months of missing Jordan from the back of his throat, but his voice still came out too gruff. "I remember." Landon and Quentin had competed with Reed on the culinary reality show, *Kitchen Wars*. They'd come in second, eliminated right after Reed and his partner, Diego. Afterwards, Landon Patton, already a rising pop star, had skyrocketed up the charts with his new album. And Quentin, his boyfriend, had opened the hottest new bakery in Los Angeles.

Reed had only gone on *Kitchen Wars* because he'd been so desperate to knit together a relationship strained by distance. A third-place finish hadn't been enough to help Reed relocate his restaurant from Chicago to LA, and after being eliminated he'd thought he'd left LA behind for good.

Now he was back, but the last person he'd ever expected to run into was Jordan.

"Landon and Quen host a cooking show called *Dream Team* for us now," Nick said, sitting down at the opposite end of the table next to a tall, blond man that Reed would have to be a lot denser not to recognize–Colin O'Connor, quarterback of the Miami Piranhas, and Nick's husband.

"We haven't met yet," a woman with long brown hair piped up. "I'm Jemma. Jemma Keane."

"Only for a few weeks longer," Landon added with excitement. "She's getting married on New Year's Day."

Reed took her outstretched hand and shook it. "Congratulations," he said, even though the word threatened to stick in his throat. He didn't want to be envious of her happiness or the way her eyes glowed, but it was inevitable when Jordan was sitting right there. He was profoundly, inescapably jealous.

He'd tried so hard not to dwell on the past. Tried not to think of what he'd lost. Looking over at Quentin and Landon, cuddled together in one seat, Nick and Colin hip to hip, and Jemma glowing with her own happiness, it was impossible to ignore the way the past pressed against him.

Suddenly it pressed too hard, and it was too big. Reed knew he had to get away and get some fresh air, even though he'd just arrived.

"I . . . uh . . . bathroom?" he stumbled. He couldn't look down at Jordan, at what was surely a knowing look in those gorgeous eyes. *He's not over me*, it would say. And Reed wasn't. Hadn't really imagined that he'd ever be, but then he'd not expected to run into Jordan anytime soon.

"Back of the building," Jemma pointed out kindly.

Trying to be honest, he did in fact go to the bathroom. He took a piss, splashed some water on his face, tried to talk himself down, but when he emerged back outside, his worst nightmare was waiting for him.

"I'm sorry," Jordan said, his hands shoved deep in the pockets of his jeans, his expression truly contrite. "I didn't know you were coming until we got here."

It wasn't Jordan's fault that he was the love of Reed's life.

"It's okay, I was just surprised." *And heartbroken all over again,* Reed didn't add.

"Not bad surprised, I hope?" Jordan asked, smiling, the corners of his eyes crinkling in genuine happiness.

I was numb without you.

"Yeah," Reed said because he didn't know what to say. Words had never been his strong suit. He could say anything he needed with his hands–by making the food that had brought them together the first time, and by touching Jordan in a million different ways.

He'd thought his actions and his creations would be enough in the end, but it wouldn't be the first or the last time Reed was wrong.

"I can go," Jordan said. "It's not a big deal." He was frowning now, the smile gone, and because Reed was hopeless, that was even worse. He'd spent so much time and energy keeping that look off Jordan's face that it felt wrong not to do the same now.

"It's been a long time. We can be adults," Reed said. "Besides, these are your friends."

Jordan brightened. "They've all been so excited to see you."

"Really?" Reed couldn't understand why. He wasn't social the same way Jordan was, like Landon and Quentin were. Even Nick had a laid-back certainty to him that Reed envied. And he wasn't even going to get started on Colin O'Connor. The man was a legend, and even though Reed's taste in football players had long run to lean ex-wide receivers with green eyes, Reed couldn't deny the man was insanely handsome.

He was just Reed Ryan. Ex-Chicagoan. Ex-restaurant owner. Drifter for the last year. Nothing special. And now he was going to be working at *Five Points*, which had begun as a sports and pop culture blog and was now recently expanding into podcasting and short videos. *Five Points'* biggest segment of growth had been in their new culinary department, especially with Landon and Quen's show, *Dream Team*. Reed had been hired to manage the test kitchen and its employees, and to produce the recipe videos and food shows *Five Points* was becoming known for. It wasn't his own restaurant exactly, but after Garnet, Reed didn't think he was ready for that yet.

The *Five Points* job had seemed like a good in-between step—ultimately working for someone else, but still managing his own kitchen.

Jordan shot him a strange look as they headed towards the front of the shack, where the food lines started. "Nick was so excited when you agreed to work for him. I think he was honestly glad that someone else was going to have to wrangle Landon and Quentin."

Right. Reed tried to shove all those annoying feelings back into the box marked, *move on*, and focus on why he was here in LA.

It probably wasn't a complete coincidence that when Reed had finally decided to settle down someplace after traveling the world for a year, he'd chosen LA. He'd not consciously thought of why Nick's job offer had seemed so attractive, but there was little doubt that deep down, he'd been wishing that he'd see Jordan again.

"You forget I watched them every week on *Kitchen Wars*," Reed pointed out. He glanced around and noticed they'd ended up in the line to order food.

"Better figure out what you want," Jordan teased kindly. "I know that'll take you awhile."

"What's good here?" Reed asked, because he was trying not to be that weird chef guy who obsessed over a new menu. Except Jordan had had a front row seat for Reed being weird chef guy, and had even claimed to find him adorable.

Jordan smiled. "Everything. You really think I forgot how you are with menus? Go on, we're not in a rush."

They weren't. The line was several people deep, and Reed was able to lose himself in the handwritten chalkboard menu.

"I spent some time in Mexico, in the Yucatan peninsula, learning about authentic Mexican food," Reed said. "These all sound amazing."

Jordan glanced over, affection still brimming out of his eyes, and it was hard for Reed to remember that they'd even broken up. If he let himself relax, nothing much had changed. "You'd better get one of everything. I know you'll regret it if you don't."

"What are you getting?"

"Probably a beer and tacos *al pastor*."

It was ingrained habit. Reed didn't know how it could be after sixteen months of separation, but then this was Jordan. He was the exception to just about every rule. "You'd probably love the torta *al pastor.*"

Turning his direction, Jordan grinned wide and looked so god damned handsome it took Reed's breath away for a moment, like his smile had just punched him right in the solar plexus. "How do you do that?"

Reed knew he could continue to be even more socially awkward than normal, or he could just own up to how things were. "I know you," he said softly. "I know food. It isn't hard to combine the two."

"You did it when you didn't even know me," Jordan pointed out wryly.

There was owning his feelings, and then there was admitting to Jordan *after* they'd been broken up for over a year that from the first moment, Reed had felt like he'd known him. That it had been easy to figure out what he liked to eat; that it came as natural as breathing. That once he'd wrapped his head around the concept that Jordan Christensen was interested in *him*, everything had been terrifyingly simple.

Sometimes love was an inevitability.

"I've always known you," Reed said, even though he knew he shouldn't.

Jordan was staring, but it was their turn to order, so Reed stepped to the register. He was grateful for a distraction from the uncomfortable truth he'd just confessed.

Reed rattled off half a dozen taco choices, added in a bucket of Coronitas, some fresh chips and salsa–"The hot kind, please," Reed requested–and then not even sparing a glance at Jordan, finished his order with the *al pastor* torta and a Dos Equis because Jordan didn't like Coronas, at least not with Mexican food.

He was just about to pull out his wallet when Jordan stepped up and slid a few twenties across the counter. "Keep the change," he told the young girl taking orders, flashing her one of his NFL football player smiles.

"You didn't need to do that, you know," Reed said as they walked to the table. "I could've gotten it."

Jordan shrugged, as laid-back with the money he'd amassed as a professional football player as he'd ever been. Not that he'd ever been super rich, like some of the more famous players were, but he'd done very well for himself. Reed had never been comfortable with it.

Reed's discomfort with Jordan's money would have been one of those difficulties they would've had to tackle as a couple if their developing relationship hadn't been rudely interrupted five months in by Jordan's trade to the Los Angeles Rams.

Instead, they'd had to fast-forward the conversation and approach the subject before Reed had been ready to. It hadn't gone well, and it had led to Reed signing on for *Kitchen Wars* to try to raise the capital to start a new restaurant in LA.

But without the cash he didn't win on *Kitchen Wars*, and without Jordan's investment as a silent partner, he hadn't been able to create a West Coast version of Garnet. After they'd been eliminated off the show, Reed had been devastated, but later, he'd realized that an LA-based Garnet never would have worked.

It was one of the reasons he'd closed the original version when he'd gone back to Chicago, and then spent the next year traveling, trying to round out his culinary experience.

Garnet had been special. The first place that had been his own. The first place he was able to truly express his own culinary ideas. But he'd gotten stale and complacent and too certain of his own success.

The *Kitchen Wars* experiment had been a painful reminder that Reed wasn't perfect. Far from it, in fact.

"I know you could have gotten it," Jordan said as they neared the table where the rest of the group sat. "But Nick gave me the cash. This is *Five Points'* treat, sort of a welcome to the team gesture."

"Thanks for the food," Reed said to Nick when he took his seat next to him. He couldn't help but notice that the others had moved down in the interim and there was no longer an empty seat for Jordan on the end. There was only the spot left next to Reed.

Not for the first time, Reed wondered what Jordan had told the others about their past relationship.

"We're really happy you're here," Nick said, sounding very sincere. "Wrangling Landon isn't for the faint of heart. You know what he's like and you're still here."

Reed knew a lot of people considered Landon Patton a handful. He was loud, he talked a lot, and he liked to have his fingers in everything. But Reed, who was quieter and much more focused, had always admired the pop star for his irrepressible spirit and personality.

"Landon," he said, trying for a teasing tone, "I think you should know that everyone keeps trying to get rid of you." It was unlike Reed to make a joke like this, but he wanted Landon–and by extension, Quentin–to know he was a hundred percent on their side. Landon and Quen were *his* talent now. He was not only the culinary manager at *Five Points*, he was also a producer of their show.

Landon gave an exaggerated sigh. "It might have been the five or six times I mentioned blowjobs when we filmed last."

A woman passing by their table did a double take at his loud exclamation and shot him a dirty look. Landon shot one right back.

"See?" Nick said casually. "We can't even take him out in public. Like I said, you'll have your hands full."

"I'm looking forward to it. It'll be good to have a base kitchen again, be able to focus on perfecting some of the recipes I picked up while traveling."

"So you spent the last . . . year . . . on the road?" It was the first time Colin had inserted himself into the conversation, and Reed told himself it was fine. It was okay. He had met NFL players before. Okay, no NFL players as famous as Colin O'Connor, but he could handle himself. He could control his social anxiety and not let it control him.

"I wanted to travel, expand my horizons," Reed explained. "It's so easy to lose sight of what's new and innovative and fresh. I'd had Garnet open for almost five years. I think I got lazy."

"You? Lazy?" Jordan scoffed.

If anyone thought it was awkward that Jordan showed zero compunction about referring to their prior relationship, they didn't show it. Instead, they peppered Reed with questions about his travels as he took big bites of some of the best tacos he'd ever had.

"Where was your favorite place?" Jemma asked as she sipped her beer.

"Thailand, definitely," Reed said. "The culinary history and the freshness of the ingredients and the incredible techniques. I loved it from the first moment I set foot in Bangkok."

"So I'm guessing you learned about more than just pad thai," Nick said.

"The breadth of their traditional dishes is . . . in the States, we don't even have a clue," Reed said. "I could've studied there for years and learned only a fraction of what they have to teach."

It was also scary easy to slip back into old habits with Jordan. Scary easy to lean over and ask him how the torta was.

Jordan was closer than Reed realized, green eyes glowing in the dusk. "It was fantastic, just like you knew it would be," he retorted with clear affection.

Reed finished his third beer and his fifth taco. He didn't usually drink much, but he'd known the alcohol would help him not over-think the social part of this evening, and would help him relax around Jordan. He'd been right, but now he was afraid he was a little *too* relaxed. It was so easy to sit next to him like this, nearly thigh to thigh, and imagine that he could slip his arm around Jordan's shoulders. Hold him close like he'd done so many times before.

The problem was that Reed didn't know if Jordan meant anything other than being friendly. They'd broken up, he'd gone back to Chicago, and Jordan had never attempted to follow him or to contact him. Reed had even kept his regular phone with him while he'd traveled and made sure it was fully charged and on whatever Wi-Fi he could find, just in case Jordan decided to text him. But he never had.

He was just trying to make sure it wasn't awkward, Reed decided. If that was Jordan's intention, it had worked because Reed had relaxed into the evening. But it had also worked too well. It was a difficult reminder that as much as Reed wanted this to be the new normal, as much as he wanted them to grow back together, stronger than they'd been before, the likelihood of that was slim.

"What about you?" Reed asked Jordan, hoping that he'd either find out something about the man's last sixteen months or why he'd quit football when he'd certainly seemed determined to finish out his contract with the Rams.

Reed could still remember his shocked reaction when he'd logged onto the internet to check his email at some hole-in-the-wall café in Rio, only to read headline after headline about how Jordan Christensen had unexpectedly hung up his cleats for good.

Reed had hoped it wasn't because of him, but also wasn't sure if he could ask.

"What about me?" Jordan teased back, which sent Reed's pulse thudding like the bass at an all-night rave. "What did you want to know?"

Of course, it was then the lights flickered over the table, and Nick got up, followed closely by his husband, then Landon, Quentin and Jemma. "Place's shutting down for the night. We'd better get going," he said casually. Like Reed and Jordan hadn't just been on the precipice of *something*. Reed didn't even know what it was, only that it had seemed important, if only because of the way Jordan had deflected the question. Jordan didn't usually deflect. Jordan always faced things head-on. It was something Reed had always admired about him.

"Hey, Jordan, would you mind giving Reed a ride back to his place? I'm going back to our house up by Malibu, and it's in the opposite direction."

Reed was not even the tiniest bit surprised that Colin and Nick owned a house near Malibu. It was only then that it occurred to him that if Jordan said yes, they'd be alone together. In a car. And if LA traffic was as advertised, it could be an uncomfortably long trip.

"Sure," Jordan said with no concern whatsoever.

Reed didn't know what he was playing at, but he wanted to shake him. Didn't he get that he'd been put on this planet to drive Reed Ryan specifically crazy? Didn't he understand that every single thing he did was an unspoken, almost certainly unconscious invitation for Reed to lose his heart over him all over again? He must not realize, or else he wouldn't be doing it.

That was how Reed ended up in Jordan's late-model Lexus. In Chicago, he had owned a similarly luxurious car, though this was different than the Range Rover he'd driven by necessity in the Midwest's brutal winters.

Jordan had clearly upgraded since moving to LA, and Reed burned with the need to ask if he'd upgraded boyfriends too. Not once during the evening had Jordan mentioned a significant other, and the rest of the group hadn't either. It seemed difficult for Reed to believe that after all this time, Jordan was still single. He was handsome and successful and charming. Reed being single wasn't a big surprise—after all, he'd been single for years before he'd met Jordan.

As Jordan pulled onto the highway, he asked, "What do you think of the place Nick found for you?"

Reed had barely had time to move his bags in and unpack the boxes of kitchen equipment he'd asked his old sous-chef *to* ship from Chicago. But the upper-floor loft with its open layout and spacious kitchen had been perfect from the first moment Reed had seen it. As he'd run his hands across the butcher block and concrete countertops, he'd imagined that Nick must have asked Quentin or another professional chef for advice in selecting the loft. But Reed had a sudden thought that maybe it hadn't been Quentin who'd given his input after all.

The loft, while bigger than the place Reed had lived in Chicago, was undeniably similar.

"I love it. And you knew I would." Reed figured that Jordan hadn't hesitated to point out how intimately Reed knew his stomach. Whether he still cared about him or not, it was also undeniable that Jordan still knew Reed just as well.

"I wondered how long that would take you."

"Not long," Reed said.

"I really don't want this to be weird between us. I figured we parted ways . . . not horribly."

Not horribly. If that meant because Reed had been a flat, contained wall shielding the cataclysm of emotions that swirled inside him those last few days in LA, then Jordan wasn't wrong. But Reed didn't know that Jordan hadn't seen through Reed's attempt to hold all the pain at bay.

Maybe he'd believed Reed was cold and unfeeling. Maybe he'd thought Reed didn't care about him after all. Maybe that was why Jordan hadn't contacted him after he'd left LA.

Reed wanted to ask, to set the record straight, but the lump in his throat made it hard to speak at all.

"It's not weird," was all he managed to get out.

"Yeah," Jordan said, glancing over, a soft smile on his face, "it's actually really nice."

That was the only warning Reed had that when Jordan pulled into the lot of Reed's building, he would actually pull into a parking space, turn the car off, and glance over at him, a knowing smile on his face.

"Do you want me to come up?" Jordan asked.

Did he want Jordan to come up?

"I know it's been a long time, almost a year and a half, and we don't have to do anything, but well," Jordan said, shooting him an apologetic smile in between his rambling, "it's been awhile for me, and it was always good between us, yeah?"

Reed thought it had been very obvious when they met and he'd told Jordan that he hadn't slept with a man in nearly two years that he didn't really do casual sex. It was a minefield for someone who suffered from social anxiety, and so he'd avoided it. Also, he just didn't like it. When he had sex with someone, he wanted it to be more than just scratching an itch.

But having sex with Jordan wouldn't just be scratching an itch. Could anything be just casual between them? He didn't know about Jordan, but on his end it was impossible. But from the way

Jordan had phrased the offer, it seemed like there hadn't been any strings attached. Just a way to get off.

"I . . ." Reed kept his eyes glued to the dashboard because if he looked over, it was inevitable that all the emotions would be right there on his face. How much he'd missed Jordan. How much he still loved him. How much he'd like nothing better than to take Jordan's hand and lead him upstairs to his bed. How much he'd like to start over, and try to move past everything that had gone wrong after such a promising start to their relationship.

"I can't. I'm sorry." Reed's eyes burned. He finally glanced over at Jordan, and to say the other man was surprised was an understatement. It was clear that he'd never believed that Reed would turn him down.

"I can't do it like this, not with you," Reed admitted lowly. "It means more to me than that. *You* mean more to me."

"Oh. *Oh.*" Comprehension was dawning on Jordan's face. How could he believe that Reed wasn't still crazy about him? Yeah, it had been sixteen months since they'd seen each other, but Reed had been head over heels for him when they'd broken up. Love like that–life-changing love–it left a mark. It didn't just evaporate if a little time had passed.

"I'll go," Reed said. "I'm sorry if that'll make it awkward next time we run into each other." He opened the door, but before he could climb out of the car, he felt a soft hand on his shoulder.

Turning back to Jordan, Reed was amazed to see such a bright, happy smile on Jordan's face. Like he'd just heard the best news ever. "Hey, have a good first day tomorrow. Nobody deserves it more than you."

CHAPTER TWO

"*So, how did it* go?" Landon hissed, leaning over the top of Jordan's cubicle.

There weren't many people who understood why an NFL player would quit his job and go to work in what was essentially a box every day.

Landon had won Jordan's endless gratitude and loyalty by simply assuming that Jordan had done it because he wanted to, and left it at that. Jordan was also grateful for the friendship that Landon and Quentin had offered so effortlessly when he'd been lonely and needed friends so badly.

And without the priceless opportunity to help craft lines for their short cooking show, *Dream Team*, Jordan wasn't sure he'd still be working at *Five Points*. Nick might have hired him, but Landon and Quentin had opened themselves up to him, and given him a glimpse of the reality behind the hottest new power couple in LA.

Jordan glanced up at Landon, who, even on his best behavior, wasn't exactly quiet. "Keep it down," he hissed right back. "Reed will be here any minute."

"That's why you need to tell me how it went *now*," Landon said.

Jordan really didn't want to tell Landon that instead of playing it cool, laid-back and relaxed like they'd talked about ahead of time, he'd become stupidly anxious and self-conscious and had tried to seduce Reed in an attempt to discover whether he still cared.

It hadn't been Jordan's finest moment.

Everyone always thought he was cool and charming; not exactly Prince Charming on his white steed, but his best friend, who had way less pressure and far more opportunity. Jordan didn't know how he'd managed to fool so many people; he was a shitty actor.

Not as shitty as Landon, though.

"It didn't go well, did it?" Landon asked, trying to hold onto the hopefulness in his expression but Jordan could see it dying faster than any inhibitions within a ten-mile radius of Landon and his boyfriend.

"There were positive points," Jordan said. The upside of asking Reed for casual sex was that he knew Reed definitely wasn't over him. But he'd known that the moment their eyes had met earlier that day.

Deep down, he'd known it the day Reed left.

If he'd had a shred of intelligence or self-preservation, he'd never have let Reed leave at all. How was he to know that instead of giving him some space, Reed would take their breakup as final, and then sell his restaurant and disappear off the face of the planet?

Jordan had never imagined that Reed had such a dramatic streak, but it definitely existed.

"And they were?" Landon prompted. He clearly wasn't ready to let this go.

Jordan looked at his watch. Fifteen minutes 'til nine, which meant they had five minutes because Reed never failed to be ten minutes early to everything.

"Let's go get some coffee."

Landon pouted. "Quen already went to get coffee."

Jordan barely held back his eye roll. "Okay, let's go get *me* some coffee. I'll tell you in the elevator."

He wasn't out at work yet, though he wasn't exactly hiding his sexuality. Jordan had a feeling that if things worked out with Reed the way he hoped they would, everyone would know he liked men sooner rather than later. Still, it probably wasn't a good idea to give Landon any opportunities to shriek loudly in the middle of the office about Jordan trying to have sex with Reed.

Landon barely waited until the elevator doors banged shut. "You did something, didn't you?" he demanded. Landon was shorter than average, with feathered dark brown hair and a pair of narrowing greenish-gray eyes. He was like a chihuahua on steroids, and Jordan loved him for it, *almost* all the time.

"Calm down, pop star," Jordan said, using the nickname he knew Landon hated. "I did do something, but I think it was good."

"Well, what is it? I'm about to die of anticipation over here."

"I asked if he wanted me to come upstairs with him." Jordan decided it might be easier to just rip the Band-Aid off.

Landon's jaw dropped and he gave Jordan a wide, congratulatory smile. The only thing that came remotely close to how much Landon enjoyed having sex with his boyfriend was hearing about other people having sex. "I told you it wouldn't take long. The very first night. I think I might have just won the pool."

"He said no," Jordan said.

"Oh. Well, *shit*." Jordan might give Landon a hard time, but he looked genuinely contrite. "I'm sorry."

The elevators dinged open. "Actually," Jordan said, "I think it was good. He said he couldn't do casual with me."

Landon nodded approvingly as they approached the Starbucks near the entrance to the building. "That's a fantastic sign. He wants *more.*"

"Jordan? Landon?"

Jordan turned around towards the front door and realized he'd miscalculated. It was Reed's first day on the job, which meant he'd be approximately thirteen minutes early.

"Oh hi, Reed," Landon said, reaching over and giving him a quick hug. Reed didn't respond to Landon, but that didn't stop Landon. Not much did. Instead, Reed continued to stare at Jordan. Almost definitely at the *Five Points* badge around his neck.

Right.

"You work here?" Reed asked incredulously.

Jordan could lie again, but that was only going to buy him a few hours, and in the end Reed would just be angrier. No, as hard as it was going to be to come clean, he needed to. He'd just wished he could have had a little more time before Reed discovered the truth.

"I do," Jordan admitted.

Landon glanced from Jordan to Reed and then back again. "Well, crap," he said. "Reed, I guess I'll see you upstairs at our meeting." And because he knew exactly what was about to happen, he split and headed for the elevators. One of Landon's smarter decisions.

Reed didn't have much of a temper, but he really didn't like being lied to. Jordan had known this when he'd agreed to the ridiculous plan that his friends had cooked up. He'd only agreed in the first place because he hadn't known how else to get Reed into his vicinity for the foreseeable future. And he'd thought that Reed would be perfect for the job Nick wanted to offer him.

But Jordan didn't think any of that was going to buy him brownie points.

"You lied," Reed said predictably, a crease forming between his brows. "Why?"

Jordan thought about telling him the complete truth. Now that he knew Reed had missed him just as much, it might be easier to say how much he still cared about him. But then Jordan remembered all the guilt he'd felt when he'd realized that he shouldn't have let Reed get away. When he should have stopped him or gone after him when he'd left LA. After he'd let too much time go by after. When he'd composed about a hundred emails and deleted them all. Just as many text messages. When he'd almost hit dial on Reed's number, more times than he could count over the last sixteen months.

He'd chickened out, every single time. He'd thought he'd get over Reed eventually, but to his own surprise, the breadth of his sadness had only deepened until he'd known for sure that what he felt for Reed was the kind of love you don't get over.

The kind you hold onto with both hands and don't let go.

The kind you pull all the stops out for if you're stupid enough to let it get away.

But he could be a little bit honest, at least. "Because the job was perfect for you and I didn't think you'd take it if you knew I worked here," Jordan said.

The crease deepened. "Did you get me the job?"

That much was easy to say and also completely true. "No. Quentin actually suggested you to Nick."

Reed shoved his hands in his pockets. "I don't know if I can believe you."

That was the hardest thing Jordan had heard yet. Harder than watching Reed escape last night. Harder than Reed turning him down, even though it had been for good reasons. Losing Reed's trust–and Jordan knew exactly how tough it was to build with him–was a killer.

"You can ask Quentin. You trust him."

Reed nodded slightly. "What did you say when Nick asked you about me?"

It was impossible to be honest now. Yes, the idea had initially been Quentin's, but then Landon had latched onto it as a way to get

Reed back around Jordan again. It was hard to discern where one plan started and the other ended. What *had* he genuinely thought the first time Landon had suggested it?

He'd wanted to laugh and to cry, both at the same time. He still wasn't sure which he felt more strongly. Probably wouldn't know until he and Reed figured out what they wanted from each other.

"I thought it could be terrible, but that it could be great too," he said.

"That sounds pretty honest." Reed still sounded doubtful, but then doubtful was his normal MO. Reed Ryan was very much a look first, leap second kind of guy, and Jordan had always loved that about him.

He loved that Reed took forever to get comfortable around people. Loved that the first time they'd ever met, Reed had casually insulted him completely by accident. He was endearing and adorable and *real*. There was nothing on earth more attractive than authenticity.

"I know I should have told you last night," Jordan admitted.

Reed glanced down at his watch and motioned to the elevator, because of course he couldn't be late. He wasn't really in danger of being late, but then he wasn't going to be early either–all because Jordan had distracted him. Jordan bit his tongue and forced himself not to apologize that he'd interfered with one of Reed's most ingrained habits.

"You should have," Reed agreed. They stepped into the elevator and it shut behind them. Jordan reached over and hit the button for the *Five Points* floor.

Reed took a deep breath that Jordan might not have heard if he wasn't so intently focused on the man next to him. "What would you have done if I'd said yes?"

Jordan turned to him in surprise. "If you'd said yes?"

Reed flushed, which was also adorable. For someone rather uninhibited in the bedroom, he could still be shy. Another thing Jordan loved. Another thing he'd missed so much that seeing it again made his heart clench. *Please tell me I can fix this*, he thought desperately.

"If we'd had sex last night."

Jordan reviewed and discarded all the flippant replies he could think of. Usually Reed wasn't such a stickler, but he'd screwed up by not telling the truth and the last thing he needed was to not take this question seriously. "Then you probably would have been angrier with me."

"But you asked me anyway," Reed stated incredulously. The elevator dinged and the doors opening, announcing their floor.

Jordan could see Nick and Jemma and some others coming towards the reception area, ready to greet their new employee. He should get lost. But he still didn't think Reed got it.

"It would have been worth it," Jordan said. "Just a kiss would have been worth it."

His bomb dropped, Jordan slipped out of the elevator, leaving Reed in the foyer, fish-mouthed as his new boss and co-workers arrived to greet him.

Yeah, he was probably going to have to apologize for that too.

Reed ground his teeth together and tried to focus as the rest of the culinary department at *Five Points* went around the table and introduced themselves.

Every person in his kitchen at Garnet had been a friend or had quickly become a friend. He didn't know how to be a boss in the traditional sense, but he needed to figure out how quick, because he was one now.

He was undeniably more flustered than he might normally be because Jordan had been throwing him curveball after curveball since last night.

First, being at the welcome dinner.

Second, suggesting they have sex.

Third, neglecting to mention that he also worked at *Five Points*.

Reed really wanted to be mad, but the truth was he was more distracted than angry. What had Jordan meant when he'd said even a single kiss would have been worth it? Considering his silence during the last sixteen months, it was impossible for Reed to believe that Jordan regretted their breakup as much as he did–but how else was he supposed to interpret his words?

"Reed," he heard as he tuned back into the meeting. "Reed, are you okay?"

Nick was looking over at him, worried expression on his face.

Reed couldn't remember the last time he'd spaced out and had been unable to hold his renowned focus. Oh yeah, the last time was when he'd been dating Jordan. "Sorry," he said. "Jet lag."

It was a terrible excuse, and not even an accurate one, but everyone around the table nodded with understanding.

"I was mentioning that you and I had talked about plans for some new series you wanted to feature at *Five Points*."

Reed gratefully grabbed onto the work Nick had dangled in front of him. Work he could do.

"The first thing I thought of was a series on techniques and tricks. Some basic stuff. Some more advanced techniques from restaurant chefs that a home cook might not know. Also, I want to expand the holiday videos you guys do, and do theme months. Especially cuisine from around the world. Make some of the more exotic recipes accessible to everyone."

As Reed glanced around the table, he saw a lot of excitement in his staff's faces. Nick had told him in one of their Skype conferences that he had an abundance of enthusiasm in his department, it just wasn't properly directed. Reed was seeing that now and it filled him with relief. He already knew he wouldn't be any good at motivating anyone to actually get involved. He'd expect that out of the gate. And it looked like that wasn't going to be an issue at all.

Reed already knew what his issue at *Five Points* was going to be.

"How're you settling in?"

Reed glanced up to see Landon leaning against the doorway to his office. Reed had been systematically going through every drawer in his desk to try to a find a pen. He'd found a ridiculous assortment of other office supplies but no pens.

"Just fine," Reed said. Landon must have taken that as an invitation because he swung his hips into the office and settled his butt down on one of the chairs by Reed's desk.

"Don't you have, I don't know, pop star things to be doing?" Reed asked. It wasn't that he didn't like Landon. He did. It was hard to *not* like Landon; he basically conned you into it and then he became addictive and you couldn't stop even if you wanted to.

Landon crossed his arms over his chest. "Jordan, Quen, and I had a meeting about the new season for our show. You should be grateful we kept you out of this one."

Reed *was* grateful. It had been exhausting enough sitting with Landon and Quentin, trying to decide the angle and direction and recipes they wanted to feature on their next batch of episodes. The first ten episodes of *Dream Team* had been a huge success, and they were both feeling extra ambitious.

Reed's job was to temper their dreams with reality, and it was definitely not easy. He'd said *budget* at least half a dozen times in their meeting alone, and knew that he'd be writing it more when he went over the notes and emphasized that they only had a certain dollar amount they could spend on food each episode.

"Why was Jordan in your meeting?" Reed asked before he could help himself.

Landon looked surprised. Which was unusual because Landon knew everything. "You didn't know that Jordan writes our scripts?"

Reed was still trying to wrap his head around the culinary side–he hadn't had the energy or the time yet to really review the production half of the equation. "You need scripts? We didn't have scripts on *Kitchen Wars*."

"Apparently I tend to ramble and make a lot of jokes that our viewers might find inappropriate," Landon sniffed.

Reed burst out laughing, because that was definitely why Landon needed a script.

"I'll have you know the scripts are awesome."

Reed didn't doubt it for a moment; Jordan excelled at anything he did, and he had the sort of irreverent humor that both Landon and Quentin liked.

"I have watched your show," Reed said instead because Landon was an enormous gossip and he didn't want to discuss Jordan with him. "You'd already been renewed when I signed on, so I knew for sure I'd be managing you two."

Landon batted his eyes. "You're a brave man, Reed Ryan."

He wasn't at all. The opposite, actually. The kind of man who ran instead of going after what he wanted. He'd never stop feeling the burn of shame that he'd failed Jordan and then ditched him instead of trying to work through it.

"You two are great," Reed said, deliberately changing the subject. "The show is great. I actually couldn't wait to work with you." He'd even stupidly imagined becoming closer friends with Landon and Quentin, only to discover when he arrived in LA that they'd already become friends with his ex.

Talk about irony.

"It was a disaster at first," Landon confided. "We were all stiff, the script was awful. It was nothing like us at all. Then Jordan watched us filming and said he could fix it. And he did."

Reed realized he must have unconsciously grimaced at Landon bringing up Jordan again, because he laid a kind hand over Reed's, and shot him a very sympathetic smile. "I know it must be really difficult," Landon said, and this time Reed made sure his expression didn't give anything away.

"Oh?" Reed asked frostily.

But Landon was incredibly tenacious, which was one thing to understand, and quite another to experience. "Rory once told me you two were even cuter than me and Quentin. So yeah, I imagine it must be really difficult."

This time Landon's voice was completely genuine.

"Rory said that?" It was impossible to snatch the question back, it was already out of Reed's mouth.

Reed remembered a snowy Chicago evening when Rory Dargan, a chef and a good friend, had stopped by Garnet, and ended up being introduced to Reed's boyfriend.

Only two months before Jordan had been traded and the whole fairy tale had come crashing around their ears.

Everything had been so different then, and it was impossible not to feel alternatively bitter and wistful when thinking about what Rory must have witnessed and passed along to Landon while they were all filming *Kitchen Wars*.

Two years earlier

"I'd heard you'd mellowed, Ryan," Rory said smugly as he shoveled pita smeared with roasted red pepper hummus into his mouth, "but imagine my shock when I come to Chicago, and you're shacked up—and not with just anyone, mind you, but with the star receiver of the Bears."

Reed blushed, embarrassed for a brief moment at how lovesick he must look for Rory to have picked up on it. *Rory,* who wouldn't notice if the Pope got married. But Jordan just laughed, sounding inordinately pleased, and wrapped an arm around Reed's shoulders. The look on Jordan's face as he gazed at him was at least as starry-eyed as Reed's own.

They were in public, tucked away behind a gigantic potted palm, at one of Reed's favorite little Mediterranean dives. Jordan had to be careful, because Chicagoans were passionate about two pastimes–football and gossip. They'd had one brief, awkward discussion about it, in which Jordan said he wasn't ready for the attention coming out publicly might bring and Reed, who didn't like attention at all and had struggled with the reveal of his own sexuality, didn't press.

Mostly it wasn't an issue. They stayed in, or when they went out, they tried to keep the touching and the besotted stares to a minimum.

Reed was okay with the former, terrible with the later. Even three months in, the concept that Jordan Christensen wanted to date *him* was wondrous. Some days it felt impossible to contain.

Tonight was one of those times, and even though Reed considered himself something above a caveman, he wanted to kiss Jordan in front of this whole restaurant and stake his claim. It would have been impossible to miss the multitude of awed looks Jordan had received tonight. He was brighter than life, with his easy laugh and charismatic grin.

"I haven't mellowed," Reed said, which was complete bullshit. He took nights off now. He smiled in the kitchen at Garnet. He let Mike, his sous-chef, pick the specials sometimes. Suddenly, Garnet, which his world had revolved around for so long, wasn't everything to Reed.

Rory burst out laughing. "You're full of shit, mate."

Jordan hadn't met many of Reed's chef friends—okay, he hadn't met *any* of them, mostly because Reed wasn't keen on asking any of them to sign the required NDA—but when Rory had unexpectedly showed up in town, it had made strangely perfect sense for Jordan to come out to dinner with them. But Jordan was used to the deference the Garnet staff showed Reed, and he could tell his boyfriend was surprised at the blunt way Rory talked to him.

"So," Rory continued, still shoving hummus into his face at an alarming rate, "how did you two meet? Because I gotta say, Reed barely sticks his head out of the kitchen for more than five minutes at a time."

"We actually met at Garnet," Jordan said, all gooey affection, like the first night they'd met, Reed hadn't accidentally insulted him.

"Oh?" Rory asked, all creamy innocence because he knew how much Reed hated being summoned to the dining room.

"It's actually really embarrassing. My agent knew how much I'd been wanting to visit Garnet, and just barged in, no reservation.

And Reed," Jordan glanced over, "was kind enough to give us the private dining room. Picked our menu for us and everything. I had to meet him, after all that trouble he went to."

Rory burst out laughing and Reed shifted uncomfortably in his chair. He had a bad feeling about where this was going.

"You realize why he actually came out of the kitchen, right? Why he picked your menu?"

Jordan shook his head, a baffled expression on his handsome face.

Rory leaned forward. "Let me educate you about the ego of a chef, Christensen. Reed didn't give you his best table and his best food out of the kindness of his heart. He did it because he wanted to put you in your place with his awesomeness."

"I'm trying to remember why I invited you out," Reed interrupted before Rory's education could continue. But Jordan, intrigued, ignored him, and Rory was never going to stop now that he'd started. Reed flopped back in his chair, somewhat resigned to the inevitable embarrassment to come.

"Reed doesn't have an ego."

Rory's head actually whipped back as he cackled loudly. "Oh, honey. All chefs do, at least the best ones. It's how we get to the top. We're insufferably certain of our own perfection. At least in the kitchen, anyway. Garnet is Reed's castle, and he's the king."

Jordan turned to Reed, who could only hold his breath and pray that Rory's comments hadn't completely changed his opinion.

"Is that true?" he asked.

"I mean, you can't be that surprised," Reed said awkwardly. "Especially after what I said when we met."

"I thought you were trying to hit on me!" Jordan exclaimed in mock outrage.

Reed flushed.

"I hate to say it," Rory said, which was a complete lie because he looked like he was enjoying every second of this, "but Reed doesn't have that kind of game."

"So, how did you two meet?" Jordan asked, and Reed wasn't dumb enough not to know he was changing the subject. He told himself it would be okay. Jordan couldn't be angry about how they'd met, so many months later.

"A butchering class," Reed said.

"No, not even close," Rory said, taking another drink from his beer. "You aren't going to get off this easy, Reed."

Reed made a disgruntled sound. Of course Rory felt obligated to tell the whole story.

"Yes, it *was* a butchering class," Rory said, gesturing with the bottle in his hand. "And you know, I'm formally trained. I mostly took it for fun. But here's Reed, a newbie who's read at least fifteen books on his own at this point. He spent at least half the class telling the instructor everything he was doing wrong."

Reed couldn't help but frown. Jordan glanced over, ever-attuned to Reed, and reached under the table to squeeze his knee.

"Was the instructor wrong?" Jordan asked loyally, even though if he knew Reed at all, he already knew the answer to his question.

Rory laughed and nodded. "Oh, he was insanely wrong. The rest of us were just ready to write this whole class off as a bad afternoon and go have some drinks later and laugh about it, but Reed was burning with the injustice of wasting an afternoon being taught what he *knew* was the wrong thing."

"So he tried to teach the class." Jordan glanced over, eyes brimming with affection. As if this story, which definitely wasn't one of the greatest moments of Reed's life, actually endeared him further.

"It was a power struggle, from beginning to end, but," Rory said, tipping the bottle in a mock toast Reed's direction, "you already know who came out on top."

"He was *wrong*," Reed felt justified in adding again.

Jordan's hand settled warm and firm back on Reed's knee. Reed jumped, nearly upsetting his own beer. "I wouldn't expect any less, sweetheart," he said quietly.

Reed wasn't used to people accepting him for who he was, social awkwardness and all. Dating Jordan was nothing like anything he'd ever experienced before—pure acceptance and love from a man who was handsome, charming and kind and could have anyone he wanted.

Later that night, as they lay in Reed's bed, damp with sweat, Reed still trying to catch his breath, Jordan rolled over and rested a possessive hand on Reed's hip.

"Just so you know, I'm really happy I read that whole night wrong," Jordan murmured. Reed's breath stuttered in his chest. "Otherwise I might not have come back, and that would have been a real shame."

Jordan's hand wandered up Reed's side and to his heart, where it pounded away beneath Reed's skin. He couldn't help it, he reached over and curled his fingers possessively over Jordan's. Holding him tight and close to his heart. "Do you really think so?"

"Someday," Jordan said, "you're finally going to see yourself the way the rest of the world sees you. The way I see you."

❧ ☙

Reed had thrown away that unconditional love like it meant nothing.

He tried to swallow the bitterness coating his tongue. Reached for the bottle of water on the corner of his desk and twisting open the top, he took a long drink. But even the water couldn't wash away his bitterness at the memory of the happy, carefree evening he'd spent with Jordan and Rory.

"Rory said it and I know he meant it," Landon said softly.

"I have a lot of work to do," Reed said, even though it was almost a lie. He did have work to do, though almost none of it was actually pressing. He needed to find a pen, and get his email set up on his laptop. Needed to read Nick's last evaluations of his department staff. But right now what he needed more than anything else was to get away from Jordan.

"Right, of course," Landon said, getting up, even though that was probably the easiest dismissal he'd ever accepted in his life. Even that galled Reed. How bad off did he look if Landon was willing to give in so easily?

"Oh," Landon said, turning back to the desk on his way out, "I forgot, I actually came by for a reason. We're having a Secret Santa exchange in the office."

"Secret Santa," Reed stated incredulously.

"Secret Santa," Landon trilled. "Christmas is only a few weeks away, you know."

"Right," Reed said, even though he'd never felt less like celebrating a holiday. No, that wasn't exactly true. He'd felt the same during every holiday since he'd left LA.

"Well, we all have to draw names," Landon said, whipping out a handful of crumpled pieces of paper out of the pocket of his tight jeans. "Here," he said extending his hand. "Pick one."

Reed grimaced. "Really?"

Landon shot Reed a reprimanding look. "We're all doing it."

It had been a long time since Reed had worked for anyone besides himself, but he figured that refusing to participate in group activities your first day on the job was probably frowned on. Even if the person organizing them was Landon Patton.

He reached over and plucked a single piece of paper from Landon's outstretched hand. He unwrapped it and stared at the name.

"Ooooh, who did you get?" Landon asked, craning his neck so he could see the writing on the paper.

"Isn't it called *Secret* Santa?" Reed asked, amused despite the fact that he was going to have to find the time to buy gifts for someone he'd barely met.

"Yes, well, it's more fun to know, don't you think?" Landon finally gave up and walked around the desk to get a better look. "Oh, you got Jemma. Well, she'll be easy, she's getting married on New Year's. Brides are easy to shop for."

Reed had never known a bride. He didn't have a clue what to get one. Maybe it was a good thing that Landon knew he'd gotten Jemma. He could beg for some advice.

"What would you get her?" he asked.

Landon looked affronted. "I couldn't *help* you!"

"You definitely should," Reed said. "I don't even know Jemma."

"Ask Jordan, they're *super* close," Landon said, as a parting gift. Or sword thrust, depending on how much credit Reed was giving Landon today.

CHAPTER THREE

TWO DAYS IN, THE biggest issue Reed was having so far was that he actually liked his new job. Which meant that despite the Jordan problem, he was not going to quit.

Quitting might have been easier. Instead he hid in his office like a chickenshit under the pretense that he was too busy to venture into the rest of the bustling office floor. Reed was about 99.9% sure that everyone who knew he'd dated Jordan—which, blessedly, was not that many yet—knew exactly why he'd barricaded himself behind his office door.

There was also the issue of the Secret Santa exchange. Twenty-four hours after drawing Jemma's name, Reed had yet to figure out what a bride might like or receive a gift himself. He knew from the email Landon had sent to the office that everyone should expect to give and receive two to three smaller gifts, and then the final larger gift during the annual Christmas party that would double as a Secret Santa reveal.

Just when Reed had come to the conclusion he was grateful because that put less pressure on the speed needed to find a gift for Jemma, he came back from one of the few meetings he had to a bright red card sitting square on his neatly organized desk.

Reed approached the envelope cautiously. His name was scrawled on the front in messy capital letters. He didn't recognize the handwriting; it definitely wasn't Jordan's. He hadn't even realized that he'd pathetically wanted to be Jordan's Secret Santa until the option was ripped away.

He sat down with a heavy sigh and reached for the envelope. It was silly to be disappointed. *Five Points* employed at least fifty people; the chances of him receiving Jordan or Jordan receiving him was slim. And yet, hope remained inextinguishable in his chest, lodged just below his breastbone.

The heavy card he slipped out was a gift certificate for six months of membership at a gym, which, Reed discovered, was very close to the apartment he rented. Walking distance, actually.

Like someone both knew where he lived and also that after a day of work, the thing he liked to do most was go to the gym and work out all his excess energy.

Of course, that hadn't been the method he'd *most* enjoyed while dating Jordan.

Reed cut that thought off hard and fast.

He wasn't going to think about Jordan. He wasn't going to think that the gift could be from Jordan. The most obvious answer wasn't necessarily the right one. Lots of people might know where he lived. *Five Points* had arranged for him to rent the apartment in the first place, and from his muscular build, it was probably very obvious that he enjoyed working out.

It was all a coincidence, nothing more.

Quentin stopped by his office near five.

"Hey," he said softly, shoving his hands in his pockets and lingering near the doorway like he wasn't sure he'd be invited inside.

Reed didn't know if his hesitation was a result of his laid-back attitude or if Reed's dismissal of Landon yesterday had made it to Quentin's ears.

Who was he kidding? This was Landon, who never stopped talking, and Quentin, who never stopped listening.

"I'm not going to bite," Reed said and Quentin flushed as he sauntered further in, dropping down in the chair opposite Reed's desk.

"This is weird," Quentin said.

"Me being your boss or you being good friends with Jordan?" Reed and Quen had never been particularly close–they had Rory in common, of course, but they'd never developed a friendship on their own.

Quen made a face that Reed was almost certain had originated in Landon's arsenal. "You're not really my boss, but it's weird anyway."

Okay, so not about Jordan. Reed pushed away his embarrassment that he'd even mentioned him. He sounded obsessed with his ex, which probably wasn't all that far from the truth.

"I'm the boss of your food budget," Reed pointed out.

"That's sort of why I'm here," Quentin said, leaning back. "I want to do an Italian dinner party episode, which means it needs to be a double episode."

"We don't have a budget for a double episode," Reed said automatically, while thinking that an Italian dinner party episode would also be golden television. Maybe this was one of those exceptions that Nick had invited Reed to bring to him when the opportunity was right.

He was right in the middle of trying to figure out how to phrase this request when Quentin said, "We want to have guests too, like a real dinner party. We were thinking you and Jordan would be perfect."

Reed laughed, because he couldn't help himself. Here he was, embarrassed about *mentioning* Jordan, when it felt like half the employees of *Five Points* were doing their best to conspire them together anyway.

"You're the most obvious choices," Quentin said, ticking off points on his fingers, like he'd rehearsed, and Reed was beginning to think he had. "You're well known from *Kitchen Wars* and even though he's retired now, Jordan is still high profile. Colin is *too* high profile, or we'd invite him and Nick. And you're both great in front of a camera–well, you have experience anyway." Quentin shot him an apologetic look, because while Reed might have been serviceable on *Kitchen Wars*, he hadn't set the audience on fire either, which was why he'd ended up in third place.

Reed jittered his leg under his desk and thought that even if he enjoyed the hell out of the challenge this new job presented, he also wasn't willing to spend the next few months subjected to every incredibly transparent matchmaking scheme Landon and Quentin could think up.

"Right," he said, trying to keep his voice calm. They were good reasons, which only meant that Quentin hadn't come up with this idea on his own. He wasn't sneaky enough, but his boyfriend? Landon had invented sneaky.

"I think it's a really good idea," Quentin said loyally.

"It is a good idea," Reed said, and it nearly killed him to admit it. "I'll have to talk to Nick about budgeting for a double episode. Do you have a tentative menu yet?"

"I'm still working on it. I'll send it over as soon as it's ready," Quentin promised, which was the final bit of evidence that Reed needed that the whole thing was a setup. A good idea but also a setup. Quen had built all their episode ideas around already complete recipes. It was unusual for him or Landon to have an episode theme first.

For Quentin, the food always came first.

Staring at the other man, Reed found he couldn't really blame Quentin. When he'd been deliriously happy with Jordan, he'd wanted to spread all that love and happiness around and let it soak into the general populace the way you soaked ladyfingers in espresso when you made tiramisu.

"You should make tiramisu for dessert," Reed suggested, because why the hell not.

Quentin's eyes lit up. "Oh god, Landon loves tiramisu."

"Exactly," Reed said. "Everyone loves tiramisu."

He didn't mention who loved it more than just about anyone else, but the ghost of him lingered in Reed's mind, the way he always did. Even though Reed had left Jordan, he'd never really left Reed.

Love was funny that way.

Jordan sat in the circular driveway of the new house in the Hollywood Hills that Landon and Quentin had just bought, and tried not to be a sweating wreck.

He already knew how Reed was going to react when he realized Jordan was coming to the Christmas movie marathon that Landon and Quen were throwing. He was so hyper-aware of the other man that he'd felt every second of his avoidance the last two days. It shouldn't have hurt, but it did, because it drove home just how much Jordan had hurt him by not going after him when he'd left LA.

He'd royally fucked up, and Jordan wasn't sure he was going to get the chance to fix it.

"Come twenty minutes late," Landon had suggested earlier that day when they'd discussed the party. "Reed will be early, and he's so polite that he won't want to duck out just because you're there."

Landon wasn't wrong, but there was a part of Jordan, the masochistic side that had enjoyed the brutal two-a-days and the hard-hitting, fast pace of the NFL, that wondered if maybe he had made his bed and he should just lie in it.

They'd hurt each other so much, and it didn't even matter whose fault it was. Maybe it was foolish to imagine he could recreate the carefree love they'd once experienced.

It was the thought that he'd never laugh with Reed again, never rest his head in the crook of his neck, never have Reed feed him breakfast in bed again—those were the painful potentials that got him out of the car and up the drive.

Landon opened the door on the first knock, like he'd been expecting him. "You're three minutes late," he hissed under his breath.

Jordan shot his friend a quelling look. "What a great place you have here, Landon," he said loudly. "That music thing must be paying off."

Landon smacked him on the arm. Hard. "Yeah, two number one singles didn't tip you off or anything," he grumbled.

"Yes, we all know you're super famous now, pop star," Jordan said, earning him another glare as they walked through the two-story foyer and into a spacious living room. A bunch of people were lounging on couches, snacking on a huge buffet of junk food that was spread out on the coffee table. Jordan saw Nick and Colin, Gabe and Jemma, and even Rory and his girlfriend, Kimber. But the only person he cared about was smiling at the TV, eyes crinkled the way they did when he thought something was really funny.

Bing Crosby and Danny Kaye were on the gigantic screen, dressed in blue sequins and singing about being sisters.

"Sorry I'm late," Jordan said belatedly, because his mother had drilled manners into him from a very young age, and given him a refresher every few years, so he wouldn't "forget where he came from." He knew the moment Reed's amusement at the characters' antics ended and he realized Jordan was there. He stiffened and the smile evaporated.

The self-recriminating asshole inside him screamed that he shouldn't continue to subject Reed to his presence when it clearly bothered him so much.

The other asshole part of him enjoyed every awkward line of Reed's body because it meant he was still affected. Still had feelings. Which added up to the fact that Jordan, after much groveling, might have a shot in hell of winning him back.

Everyone else in the room looked up with a genuine smile, happy to see him. Only Reed continued to frown.

"Here, I saved you a seat," Landon said, bustling between the packed sofa and the loaded coffee table. "Did you want a beer?" He stopped at the minuscule sliver of space between the edge of the sofa and Reed, who glanced up like a deer caught in Landon's headlights.

Shit. Jordan knew Landon tended to get carried away with things, and he'd still let him loose on this plan like he didn't have a very good idea of the consequences.

"Your sofa is like a mushy sponge," Jordan said, "I'll sit on the floor. It'll be better for my back."

"I keep telling you that," Quentin seconded. Jordan didn't know if Quen actually thought the sofa was horribly uncomfortable–which it was–or if he was just trying to help Jordan out, but he was grateful regardless.

"Fine," Landon sniffed. "You can get your own beer, then." He settled back into his own seat, which was Quentin's lap.

"Here, I'm about to go grab one, I'll get you one," Nick said, shooting Jordan a sympathetic look as he got up and headed towards the kitchen.

The problem was even though he was sitting on the floor, back against the edge of the sofa, Jordan found it was impossible to focus on the movie or forget that Reed was only a few inches away. And from the way Reed was fidgeting, leaning over to grab snacks from the coffee table, shifting his position every few minutes, it was clear he felt the same way.

Landon must have noticed because at the end of one of the bigger musical numbers, he pointedly glanced over at Reed. "Sure I can't get you anything, Reed?" he asked, and the man flushed. Jordan couldn't help but glare over at his friend, because of course Landon didn't just let things alone. He had to interfere.

"I'm fine," Reed stuttered. And then he said something that shocked Jordan. Reed had been surprising him from the first time they'd met, but this felt different. Reed turned to him. "You really should come sit up here. I can't enjoy this movie knowing you're on the floor. Especially when I know your back bothers you sometimes."

Jordan carefully avoided looking at what was surely a triumphant expression on Landon's face. He had to face the possibility that maybe Reed's actions hadn't been because Jordan made him uncomfortable, but instead that he'd been worried about Jordan's comfort.

"And you can reach these snacks better," Reed said. "If we have to watch two clearly gay men pretend to fall in love with these nice ladies, you need to try these homemade crackers with the fig jam. And a little slice of the brie."

It was hard not to look smug as he squished in next to Reed, especially since as soon as he was settled on the couch, Reed had already started piling food on a plate for him. Reed had always loved feeding him and, clearly, that hadn't changed.

"I'm going to pretend you didn't say that, Ryan," Landon sniffed. "*White Christmas* is one of my favorite movies."

Colin, who had been mostly silent up to this point, laughed. "I mean, he's pretty much right."

"*Sisters?*" Nick asked archly, and the whole group descended into giggles.

"This is a holiday classic," Landon argued.

"I like it," Quentin said loyally.

Jordan rolled his eyes and in response, hissed out a whipping noise, sending everyone in the room into more laughter.

"Maybe, but at least I'm not as whipped as Bing Crosby," Quentin retorted.

"Point," Colin said, wrapping an arm around Nick and pulling him in closer, which, Jordan didn't miss, gave Reed and as a result, Jordan, a little bit more room.

Except that Jordan wanted to continue to be squished thigh to thigh with Reed. He'd happily be plastered head to toe with him, if he could. He still smelled the same, like smoky vanilla, and still radiated warmth from his solid, muscular body.

Jordan had sort of expected him to lose some of his muscle tone while he was traveling the world, because he wouldn't need to expend his energy after work the same way. And who knew what kind of facilities he would find wherever he was. But he was just as built as ever, and it turned Jordan on as much as it ever had.

It was impossible to forget his first reaction to Reed—he'd been struck dumb by how his biceps and pecs strained his chef's jacket, and how kind his dark eyes were, even as he'd told them they'd needed a reservation. Jordan hadn't cared and had barely noticed. He'd been distracted by how every molecule in his body perked up and pointed in Reed's direction. It was the kind of visceral re-action Jordan hadn't experienced with many men, and it was the strongest it had ever been with Reed.

He'd been thrown at first, worried that maybe it had been one-sided, but then he'd come back on a whim to Garnet, making sure to call first, and then he'd come back again. And Jordan had known when he'd invited Reed to have dessert with him that he wasn't alone.

He flustered Reed as much as Reed flustered him, and the knowl-edge was even sweeter than the dessert they'd shared that first night.

It was the stupidest excuse on the planet. *He couldn't watch the movie if Jordan was sitting on the floor?*

Reed knew he should feel ashamed for such a transparent ruse, but if he was pressed next to Jordan, he didn't really care. Besides, it was hard to miss how most of the people in this room were actively trying to push him and Jordan together.

It had occurred to him, as he'd spent most of the last hour watching the stiff line of Jordan's back rather than the unfolding drama on the screen, that being Jordan's friends, they would know better than anyone if he was interested in getting back together.

Landon might be thoughtless at times, but he wasn't cruel. He wouldn't be doing this if he didn't think it would work out again.

Which left Reed both relieved–the nightmare of the last sixteen months was finally over, and he could work on rebuilding his life with Jordan back in it–and also terrified. If Jordan cared so much, why hadn't he followed Reed to Chicago? Why hadn't he contacted him at all?

Why wait until now?

There were little pockets of bitter hurt buried in the midst of the relief Reed felt. Was it as easy as simply listening to Jordan's apology? Was it as easy as apologizing for his own role in the fiasco that was their post-*Kitchen Wars* life?

Reed didn't know.

So Reed defaulted to the one thing he understood—food.

Pairing things he knew Jordan would like with his own choices, he kept their plate piled high. The first time he'd nudged Jordan with his own shoulder, indicating the plate with a glance, Reed swore Jordan's fingers trembled as they'd picked a cube of cheese from the edge closest to him.

They'd shared plates plenty of times. He had so many memories of piling food onto a plate and them sharing it in front of the TV on Jordan's insanely comfortable couch or Reed's own slightly less comfortable version.

Maybe it was just that easy to merge back together as if the last sixteen months hadn't happened.

Except Rosemary Clooney happened.

Standing in her dramatic black dress, looking like the world's most fabulous widow, she sung about how love hadn't done right by her. And it was so much the litany of anger and frustration and pain that Reed had been through that his heart ached.

Because he'd never really blamed Jordan. Hadn't really blamed himself. It had been so much easier to blame the emotion that had carried Reed right along with it.

When the song ended, Reed could barely clear the bitterness out of the back of his throat to ask Landon where the bathroom was.

He passed it and instead slid open the back veranda door, stepping out into the warm night air. The deck was clearly intended for both entertaining, with its grouped sections of casual outdoor furniture, and romance, with two of the chairs clustered around a fire pit at the opposite end.

His heart burned with injustice despite all his good intentions. It had been hard to see Landon and Quentin grow so close during *Kitchen Wars* while his own relationship had only splintered further, the silence that had replaced the laughter growing deeper and colder the longer he spent in LA.

Reed plopped down on a cushioned chair overlooking the Hollywood Hills, forcing himself to acknowledge that Jordan still caring about him hadn't automatically mended his still-broken heart.

The door slid open behind him, and he glanced back, dreading that Jordan had followed him out there. He always wanted to see him, but right now, everything felt a little too tender. Too exposed. At the best of times he wasn't good with words, and he definitely might say something he would regret tonight.

But it wasn't Jordan. It was Colin.

He shoved his hands into the pockets of his jeans and wandered over to the railing, leaning on it, his hair burnished gold in the setting California sun.

They'd barely exchanged more than a handful of words since they'd met, but it was too much of a coincidence to hope that Colin hadn't been sent out here to find him.

"Hey," Colin said, voice kind. "You okay?"

Reed shrugged. He didn't ever like talking about his feelings, and he definitely wasn't going to do it with someone he'd barely met. Especially since that person happened to be a very famous quarterback.

"You get sent to retrieve me?" Reed asked a little bitterly.

"Sort of." Colin hesitated a moment. "I sent myself."

That was a surprise. It must have shown on Reed's face because Colin chuckled.

"I'm assuming you've realized this is one of many opportunities to force you and Jordan into the same room," Colin continued. "And if you need a break or need them to cut it out, it's your right to say so. Your relationship, past and present, is between you and Jordan."

Colin wasn't wrong. The problem was the thought of Jordan continually choosing to put them in the same room together made it hard for Reed to breathe. Too many emotions warring inside him.

Too much. Too soon. All liable to send him into something he'd never gotten before sixteen months ago–a panic attack.

"I'm not sure I'm ready for him to choose to put us in the same room together," Reed said wryly. He hadn't even meant to say it. But Colin had a calming, quiet presence about him that made him shockingly easy to confide in.

"Love is terrifying. Sometimes it feels like the best and worst thing that can happen to you," Colin admitted.

Reed shot the man next to him a confused look. Colin and Nick had a famously happy marriage. "The worst thing?" he asked incredulously.

Colin laughed. "I know, it doesn't seem like that now. But if the person I'd cared about before Nick had ever returned my feelings, I think my life would have turned out very different. In the end, the tough times just made me fight harder for what I wanted when I found it."

"Nick."

"I wish I could tell you that I wanted him from the first moment we met, but that would be a lie. What about you and Jordan?"

Reed wished he had a better story to tell. "I actually insulted him the first time we met. Luckily he didn't realize it at the time, and thought I was just trying to hit on him." Reed paused, considering. "But after that, it was pretty much perfect. Maybe too perfect.

When he got traded, we hadn't been together long enough to figure out what to do in a crisis."

"A crisis?" Colin raised an eyebrow. "He was traded. A little long distance doesn't kill anyone."

Reed still didn't think he could communicate the sheer panic he'd felt when Jordan had told him. "I know. I realized that way too late. But at the time, all I could think was that this perfect bubble of love we'd created was going to end, and I'd do anything to keep it intact. I'd . . . not dated much, before him. Maybe if I had, I would have realized that the bubble was always going to burst."

"It's none of my business, but have you ever thought about telling Jordan that?" Colin asked.

"After *Kitchen Wars*, I ran away, back to Chicago. Panicked. Frustrated that I'd lost. Couldn't fall back into old habits without Jordan anymore. So packed everything, sold Garnet, and left. Didn't really give myself much time to tell him." Reed knew how bleak he sounded. How guilty. He'd always blamed Jordan for never coming after him, but he'd been the first to cut and run. He'd been the one to freak out about the possibility of a long-distance relationship. After everything he'd done pushing Jordan away, who could blame him for not following?

Reed couldn't. Not anymore.

Up until now, it had felt like they both held equal blame for the relationship falling apart, but after talking it through with Colin, Reed realized just how much he'd fucked up.

"You should tell him," Colin said. "One time early in our relationship, Nick was really stupid. And I knew it, even though he'd hurt me. For a week or two I thought about just letting him stew in his own stupidness, but then I realized I was punishing myself too. So I told him exactly how stupid he was."

"We've been stewing in stupidness for over a year," Reed admitted.

Colin's glance over at him was painful in its bluntness. "Time to stop stewing then."

Jordan had no idea where Reed had disappeared to, and even though he knew it wasn't fair, he still wasn't happy about it. The movie was winding to a close, the white part of the title actually falling from the sky as everyone finally hooked up.

He had to admit that Colin was probably right; the two main characters would have been happier together than with who they'd ended up. Despite that growing belief, Jordan had tried to stay interested in the movie even after Reed had suddenly disappeared and then never re-appeared. Consoling himself with the fact that Landon and Quen's house was ridiculously large and it was probably easy to get lost or distracted, Jordan also told himself that it was no business of his what Reed did with his time.

That hurt, but it was the bracing sort of pain. Before, Jordan had let Reed just *leave*, and had done almost nothing to stop it. He couldn't do that again. Maybe it was time to make sure Reed hadn't gotten lost in Landon and Quen's sex dungeon, because that was definitely something that existed. Jordan was still trying to bleach the thought out of his brain after hearing them talk about it in a meeting last year.

"Anyone see where Reed went off to?" Jordan asked, no longer caring if he was transparent. He cared where his ex-boyfriend went to—it wasn't a capital offense and he needed to stop being so embarrassed about that particular fact.

"I think he went to the bathroom?" Landon said, wrinkling his nose.

Jordan took the info and definitely wasn't going to disclose that Reed had left at least twenty minutes ago, and he hadn't been in the bathroom all that time. Instead, he decided to go wandering and see if he could wander into Reed.

He took a shortcut through the massive kitchen, with its two fridges and multiple ovens, and headed towards the back of the house to check where Landon was building himself a studio. He was just passing through a hallway when Reed opened a door and nearly fell on top of him.

Jordan was used to keeping his feet in difficult situations—catching the ball had only been part of his job—and he steadied himself automatically, reaching for Reed so he could do the same for him.

His hands went to Reed's muscular torso, fingers digging into the cotton of his t-shirt. Maybe it was muscle memory but he tugged Reed even closer. Reed's hands slid up to his shoulders, and for an eternal moment, they hung onto each other.

Reed's dark eyes were soft and yearning, and Jordan couldn't help himself. He yearned right back, fingers spreading across Reed's hard pec muscles, right where his heart thumped under his hand.

For that lingering second, Jordan could only hear the accelerated pulse of that normally steady thudding, and see the need in Reed's eyes, the wistfulness mixing with something hotter. Jordan knew he should let him go and move away, but he'd never stopped wanting this.

He'd never stopped wanting Reed.

Reed had said it could never be casual between them, and it never had been, but this moment felt momentous. Weighty. Every movement deliberate and important, whereas before they'd only been winging it. Diving in without any real concept what could happen. Now they both knew, and they both wanted it again.

It would be so easy to tilt his head down and kiss Reed again. His tongue flicked out and wet his lower lip, a nervous tick that had always caught Jordan's attention. It did now, and more. He could taste that lower lip again, it would only take a tiny movement to make it happen, and Reed wasn't pushing him away.

He'd almost decided to say *fuck it* to all his genuinely good intentions when he heard the worst sound in the world.

Slow clapping, and then, an annoyingly charming laugh.

Jordan glanced up and naturally, because he was clearly cursed, Quentin was standing in the hallway, eyes twinkling with amusement at having caught Reed and Jordan in this position. Probably also because he could tell Landon later, and Landon would eat this up.

Reed disengaged immediately when he spotted Quentin. Jordan fought back an indelible need to grab him and pull him right back, back where he belonged.

"I see you two found some of the mistletoe," Quen said, still laughing. He pointed to the top of the doorway Reed was standing in, which Jordan realized was the bathroom.

Landon had been right after all, and Landon had also apparently decked his house in mistletoe.

Jordan didn't know whether to be annoyed or grateful. Or both.

He opened his mouth to say something—*anything,* he didn't even know what, but he needed to diffuse the moment before Reed cut and ran. He'd always prided himself on thinking quick on his feet, but now the recent nearness of Reed tied his tongue until he couldn't even speak.

"Mistletoe is a parasite," Reed said tightly, his arms wrapping around his own torso. The exact spot Jordan's arms had been only a moment ago. "Shouldn't have it hanging around everywhere." And then he escaped, sliding right past Jordan before he could figure out a single fucking word to say.

"Huh," Quentin said. "I didn't know that."

Jordan rolled his eyes. "Couldn't you have just . . . I don't know . . . left silently and not started *clapping*?"

Quentin shrugged. "I was so surprised, it just happened. Hey, good news, it happened once, it'll happen again, right?"

Jordan wasn't entirely sure if that was true. But when he finally got himself under control and returned to the living room, Reed was back in the same spot and offered Jordan a hesitant smile when he approached.

Maybe Quen wasn't wrong, but Jordan wasn't going to let him forget that his boyfriend had hung parasites all over the damn house. Or that he'd never gotten the kiss he'd been entitled to.

Chapter Four

It wasn't all that easy to stop stewing, no matter how much Reed wanted to.

Two days after the Christmas movie party, Reed still found himself obsessing over the past even though he was actively trying to let it go. He'd gone grocery shopping and spent the evening perfecting one of his favorite Thai recipes, forgoing the gym for one night. He'd told himself he needed a night off.

Now, lying in bed, unable to sleep, he realized that had been a huge mistake. He couldn't get that moment in the hallway of Landon and Quen's house out of his mind. The way Jordan's hands had instinctively caught him. The way his body had closed the distance like he never wanted to be anywhere else.

Jordan had said they could keep it casual, but Reed was beginning to wonder if that was true. The serious, rapt expression on Jordan's face had hardly seemed casual. Neither had the way his fingers had spread right over where his heart had beat rapidly beneath Jordan's palm.

After endless minutes of replaying that single, breathless moment in his mind, Reed flung himself out of bed, pulled on a pair of athletic shorts and jogged down to the twenty-four-hour gym where he conveniently now had a brand-new membership. No shirt, but it was unseasonably warm for southern California in December, and it was so late, the gym would probably be empty.

It wasn't.

Reed froze in the entrance to the weight room, sure that his uncooperative mind was only playing tricks.

That *definitely* was not Jordan, back flat on the weight bench, biceps flexed as he lifted the barbell.

But Reed would know that body anywhere. The muscular slope of his shoulders, the bunch of his quads as he braced his legs on the ground, the slim tapering of his waist.

Reed would recognize that soft trail of hair leading to the low-hanging waistband of his shorts anywhere. He'd definitely traced every one of those abdominal muscles with his tongue. His mouth went dry and he could only stand and stare as Jordan finished his set of reps.

It was only instinct to glance at the weight as Jordan set the bar back on its holder above his head. He was benching more than he used to, and Reed could tell. He couldn't help but run a very appreciative eye over his ex-boyfriend's form. Jordan had always looked incredible naked, but Reed was fighting a very compelling desire to drop to his knees right between his legs and re-acquaint himself with every single ridge of muscle, every inch of exposed skin.

Jordan exhaled, the sound almost unbearably loud in the room, and Reed knew he should leave now, before something could happen that he wasn't ready for. If Quentin hadn't shown up the other day, Reed knew he would've given into the desire in Jordan's eyes. He'd felt its twin, pulsing through his own veins.

It was a weak imitation compared to what he was experiencing now.

Too many memories of them sharing a workout and then even more after were flying through his brain, Jordan bracing him against the shower wall, his length hot and hard between his cheeks, as they'd panted through the steam.

Then Jordan glanced up, their eyes meeting like two magnets drawn inexorably together. Reed froze.

"I wondered if I'd run into you here someday," Jordan said conversationally, like the air didn't feel thick with everything they'd used to do on nights just like this one.

"Yeah. I mean, I'm here. Right now." Reed knew he was stammering and stumbling, but his tongue was so thick in his mouth and his dick was so fucking thick in his shorts right now, lifting weights felt impossible.

Speaking felt impossible.

He should have known this was inevitable, from the moment Jordan had turned to him in the car that first night, eyes bright and almost careless, and offered to come upstairs.

Reed hadn't wanted it half as bad as he wanted it now, and he had wanted it damn bad then.

Jordan stood and sauntered towards him, like Reed needed any fucking reminders of how hot he was. Reed knew, and he was burning up with it. "You need a spotter?" Jordan asked.

Reed had always insisted that Jordan needed one, even when he was lazy about it. "Should've had one already," he said, because he couldn't turn off how much he cared about Jordan. Now, and always.

Jordan laughed. "You're cute." He reached out, like two days ago had acclimated them to touching each other again, and brushed the bunched muscles of Reed's shoulder. Yeah, he was tense. It felt like he was hard everywhere, and Jordan deciding to touch him again didn't help that situation any.

"Just cute?"

Jordan's gaze darkened. Reed could tell he wanted to touch again. Hell, *Reed* wanted him to touch again. He might even beg for it at this point.

"You know I think you're hot," Jordan growled, his voice rough with what had to be desire. "The first moment I ever saw you, I wanted to bend you over our table. Or maybe let you bend me. I didn't care." *And I don't care now.* He might not have said it out loud, but Reed knew exactly what Jordan meant. Even when Reed had been his most awkward self, it had still been too scorching between them to ever dream about resisting.

Why was he still resisting now? The look in Jordan's eyes was an invitation to every single act Reed had dreamt about, his hand wrapped tight around his dick, hating how poor of a substitution it was for the real thing.

Reed might pretend he didn't know why, but he knew. The rapid thumping of his heart yesterday under Jordan's palm. He didn't just want to fuck him senseless again; he wanted to lie in bed together afterwards and talk the way they used to. That was why he couldn't let himself off the self-imposed leash just yet, no matter how tightly it bound him.

Reed found his voice again. "Come on," he said, and he couldn't help the sex in his voice. It was all he was thinking about, it couldn't help but show. But that didn't mean he was giving in. "Let's lift. I couldn't sleep."

Jordan gave a short, un-amused laugh. "Yeah, me either. Can't imagine why."

Reed pinned him with a single look. "Don't. It's not funny." His heart wasn't a laughing matter.

"Believe me," Jordan agreed, his own voice growing calmer, "I think it's plenty serious."

It was Reed's first real indication that Jordan's insistence on this being "casual," was just one more front. He wanted to bury himself beneath that wall of affected, laid-back chill, and find out just how Jordan really felt.

He wasn't quite ready to have that conversation that he'd begun to think about after the talk with Colin, but he was getting closer. *They* were getting closer.

Not as close as his dick wanted to be tonight, but he'd ignored it before. He could do it again.

He'd just think about how good it would feel when he finally allowed them to give in.

2 years ago

"Here's the lavender honey thyme crème brûlée. Chef's special tonight," Dan said with a flourish as he set the *one* dessert down in the middle of the small table. Reed would have to be a lot more obtuse to miss the smug look Dan shot his direction as he sauntered away.

It was only after swallowing again, that Reed realized he'd not asked for a glass of water. And if he went back to the kitchen and grabbed one now, it would look weird. Like Jordan was making him uncomfortable, and he was, but it was a good sort of uncomfortable, a fire burning under his skin.

"Wanna try the wine?" Jordan asked, tipping the glass Reed's direction, like he knew how dry Reed's throat suddenly was.

Reed wasn't sure which was worse–sharing Jordan's wine like a lover might, or leaving to track Dan down.

The speculative glint in those fantastically green eyes sealed the deal. He reached for the wine glass, letting a good amount slide down his throat.

"It's good wine," Jordan said. "But the food is better."

"I'm a wine barbarian," Reed admitted. "I hire a sommelier to do my wine selections. I keep telling myself it's worth it to learn, but I never have the time."

"I'm a wine snob," Jordan confided, leaning closer, sending Reed's pulse into an unsteady throb. "But I'm a food elitist. Let's try this crème brûlée and see if it holds up to the rest of the dinner."

Jordan's spoon broke the sugar crust with a quick snap, and he scooped up a bit of the custard and Reed goggled as he slid the utensil into his mouth. Slowly. Explicitly. Like Reed wasn't already putty in his hands. Like he wasn't ready to give Jordan everything he wanted, as often as he wanted it.

The wine hadn't helped, but Reed reached for it again. "How is it?" he asked between sips. "Worthy of Garnet?"

The look Jordan shot him was smoky. "Absolutely. You wanna try it?"

There was only one spoon. Reed cursed and blessed Dan all in one thought. "Have to make sure it's worthy of the dessert menu," he said because he couldn't say he was dying for Jordan to stick his spoon in his mouth.

The Reed in his head that was brave and dramatic might have said something like that, dished back Jordan's flirting just as aggressively, but Reed knew he was never going to be that guy. So he just gazed at Jordan with everything he felt plainly written on his features, and hoped Jordan got the right idea.

He must have, because Jordan scooped up another mouthful and guided it towards Reed's lips.

Reed didn't even think that he hoped none of his staff or patrons were still around to witness the crème brûlée pornography. Jordan slid the spoon into his mouth, and Reed didn't think he was Jordan's equal but he tried to give as good as he'd gotten, letting the spoon slip between his lips with a last little lick of his tongue.

From the way Jordan's gaze heated up, Reed thought he'd done his goal justice.

Of course Dan reappeared a moment later. "Can I get you two anything else?" he asked solicitously, as if his boss sharing dessert with a patron wasn't completely unheard of.

"Just the check," Jordan said.

"No need," Reed asked, trying not to blush. It wasn't exactly a date, but he could still buy Jordan dinner. "We're good, thanks, Dan."

Jordan's expression was speculative as Dan disappeared. "Thank you, you didn't have to do that."

"I wanted to," Reed answered honestly. "I'd like to be able to give you more. But this is the best of me."

Jordan reached over and surprised Reed by taking his hand in his own. "I'd like that too."

"I have to help the guys clean up, in the back. But if you can stay?" Reed hoped he didn't sound as awkward as he feared. After all, they definitely seemed to be on the same page.

"There's nowhere I'd rather be."

"I'll have Dan bring you another glass of wine then," Reed said as he rose. "I think I drank all yours."

"No need," Jordan insisted. "Don't usually drink more than one glass during the season, anyway."

"Okay." Reed hovered near the table, unsure if he was being rude by abandoning him here, but knowing Mike and the others needed help cleaning up. And the sooner he was done, the sooner he and Jordan could leave and do *something* else. Reed wouldn't let his mind wander to what the *something* might be. Just spending time with the man might be enough for Reed.

"You're fine," Jordan said, giving him a little wave. "Go do your stuff. I'll be good here."

If Mike shot Reed a knowing look when he walked back in the kitchen, Reed ignored it. Luckily, his sous- chef had already started the nightly cleanup, giving orders the same way Reed would, if Reed had been present.

"I've got this, Chef," Mike said quietly.

"No," Reed insisted. "You know the rule."

The rule was, *whoever was part of the dinner service was required to help clean up.*

Besides, the idea of scrubbing off his nerves felt like a good one. So Reed went back to the big set of sinks and helped scour pans with Jack, the dishwasher.

When he looked up twenty minutes later, Mike was standing in front of him. Jack was gone. Reed was on the last pot, giving it a final rinse before setting it on the drying rack.

"All done, Chef," he said respectfully, his tone of voice not betraying one hint of surprise that there was a man still in the dining room, waiting for their leader.

Reed wiped his hands on a towel. His nerves were still dancing in the pit of his stomach, anticipation and fear warring with each other.

"Have a good night. I'll lock up."

All his staff must have known because Reed had never seen them vacate the premises so quickly.

Reed resisted the urge to go back in the bathroom and make sure he still looked presentable. He was still Reed. He hadn't gotten magically more handsome in the last twenty minutes. If Jordan had liked him before, then chances were he still would.

Jordan was on his phone, intently staring at something when Reed walked back into the dining room.

"All done," Reed said. "I just need to grab my jacket and lock up."

The look of happy anticipation on Jordan's face when he glanced up to see Reed was enough to send Reed's pulse into a fast, uneven pace.

"Can I see the kitchen first? Sorry, I'm just so curious about where all the magic happens."

Like Reed was going to deny this man anything.

"Sure. It's not very exciting though."

Jordan stood and brushed his slacks. "You say that because it's not to you," he teased as they made their way back towards the double doors. "But to us regular civilians, it's fascinating."

Reed could only stare dumbly as Jordan's eyes twinkled in the dim light.

Mike had switched the main lights of the kitchen off before he'd left, so Reed reached over and flipped them on. Jordan didn't wait for Reed to explain how it all worked, he just wandered around the different stations, seemingly fascinated by the equipment and the tools.

"You have a very clean kitchen," he observed, leaning back against one of the long stainless steel counters.

Reed felt unsure what he was supposed to do? Go over and join him? Were they not leaving? If they did leave, what would they do? Not for the first time he wished he didn't overthink every social interaction and that he'd spent more of the last few years dating because then he might not feel so lost.

Jordan smiled, and must have sensed his indecision because he patted the spot on the counter next to him. "I won't bite, I promise," he said.

Reed was perfectly happy to let Jordan set the tone and the speed and make the decisions. He was overwhelmed enough that this gorgeous man was just as riveted with him as he was his kitchen. So he walked over and tried to seem as effortlessly casual as Jordan as he leaned on the counter.

Reed was certain he failed, but Jordan smiled even wider, so he took it as a win.

"Of course I have a clean kitchen," Reed said.

"Are all chefs perfectionists?"

"I can't speak for anyone else, I just know that for *me* to be a good chef, that's what's required," Reed admitted.

"There's a level of that on the football field too," Jordan said. "If I didn't run a perfect route, the ball might not get caught, or even worse, be intercepted. And that would be on me."

Reed knew Jordan didn't do that. He'd watched enough football on Sundays to know, partially because the announcers never stopped talking about it and partially because Reed was observant, that Jordan was one of the most reliable receivers in the NFL.

"Not that it's anything similar," Jordan continued, a wry smile on his face. "I just run around a big field and catch some footballs. You create art here."

"That catch last Sunday was pretty artful," Reed retorted. "I can't imagine anyone catching that ball but you."

Jordan's eyes brightened. "You watch football?"

Reed told himself that Jordan had admitted to being a fan with a minimum of fuss. It wasn't a big deal to tell Jordan that he'd been watching–and admiring–him. "Not until a few years ago." Reed could still barely get the words out and he knew he was blushing. "You're just a really exciting player to watch."

The bashful smile that Jordan shot him was sweeter than the dessert they'd shared. Reed noticed Jordan slide a little closer, and forced himself not to instinctually move away. It was *good* they were getting close. It was just so long since he'd let a cute boy get this close. His heart was thundering under his thin t-shirt and he couldn't believe Jordan hadn't noticed it yet.

"I guess we're both fans of each other. It's surprising that we haven't crossed paths yet. Chicago is big, but it's small too, sometimes."

Reed couldn't tell Jordan that if he hadn't shown up at Garnet, he never would have sought the other man out. That wasn't how he worked.

"For example," Jordan continued, sliding even closer, until their legs brushed together, "if I'd known you looked like this, I would have come around a hell of a lot sooner."

Reed swallowed hard. "I'm just me."

Jordan was taller. In a single, impossibly quick, graceful motion, he had Reed neatly boxed in against the counter. "And you don't have a clue how impossibly attractive that is, do you?"

Reed just shook his head. It occurred to him, then, right as Jordan began to lean down, that he hadn't said the important thing he'd decided while scouring the pots. He didn't know much about Jordan personally, but of course, he'd heard about the behavior of some NFL players. That they . . . played the other field too. And Reed, who was already in the weeds, wasn't going to be able to handle that. He couldn't have one taste and then lose it forever.

"Will you go to dinner with me sometime?" Reed said before he could chicken out. Jordan's eyes, which had nearly fluttered close, popped back open. But he didn't look upset. He just smiled wide.

"Yes. In fact, I thought you'd never ask," Jordan said decisively. He shifted his weight, and for the first time, Reed caught a glimpse of the nerves hiding behind his assured exterior. The way his pulse fluttered in his neck. The uneasiness hidden in his eyes.

Reed only liked him more for it. It made him more real, more *human*. Less Jordan Christensen, NFL player, and more Jordan Christensen, the guy Reed might be dating.

"Good," Reed said, wetting his lips with his tongue. Jordan's face was so close, and for the first time in ages, Reed didn't want to push someone away. He wanted to pull him closer. So he did.

He'd been right—he *did* have to reach up to kiss Jordan, their lips brushing together once, then twice, gentle and slow. Reed had started the kiss, but it still wasn't like he'd imagined Jordan kissed.

Because he had definitely imagined how Jordan Christensen might kiss, long before he'd ever walked into Garnet.

His shoulders were warm and broad under his polo shirt, the tanned skin of his neck shockingly soft under Reed's fingers as he let them brush under the collar.

Jordan made a shocked, happy noise and kissed Reed again. Deeper. Wetter. His tongue flickering against Reed's until he felt lightheaded.

The kiss ended and Reed couldn't help but pant into the curve of Jordan's neck.

"You're so god damned perfect," Jordan whispered and Reed closed his eyes against the wave of emotions that he couldn't have braced against if he'd had a thousand years to prepare. Jordan swept them all away, like any hesitation, any concern, any holding back, didn't exist to him, and it shouldn't exist for Reed either.

CHAPTER FIVE

PRESENT DAY

"I didn't think you drank coffee," a voice behind Reed said.

Not just a voice. Jordan.

Of course Reed wasn't really surprised Jordan was here. He'd deliberately gone to the Starbucks on the ground floor of the *Five Points* office building, specifically at the time when he'd observed Jordan taking most of his mid-morning coffee breaks.

He'd told himself that he was sort of lying in wait for his ex-boyfriend for a good reason, but there were other people he could have asked for advice.

"I still don't," Reed said wryly, turning to face Jordan.

"You do realize you're in the temple of coffee, right?"

"It's not for me," Reed admitted. "I'm trying to find something Jemma might like for the Secret Santa exchange."

Jordan crossed his arms over his chest, but still grinned irrepressibly. The same old Jordan. Reed's heart ached a little. Not quite the way his dick had ached a few nights before when they'd run into each other at the gym, but Reed wanted all of him, so it made sense he made every part of Reed ache. "I thought that was supposed to be secret."

Reed made a face. "Yeah, it is when you actually know the person you're supposed to buy gifts for."

"So you need help?" Jordan asked. He wasn't stupid–Reed only hoped that he wouldn't figure out that he'd ambushed him, instead of simply asking for help like any normal person might.

"I'm lost," Reed admitted, gesturing to the loaded shelves full of holiday-themed Starbucks memorabilia. "I've been debating if gift cards are just too impersonal, but how can I do any better?"

"Unless you're a mind reader, I don't see how you possibly could. Well, I'll tell you that Jemma likes her coffee strong and sweet and cold. Like ice-cold. Which is a weird-ass habit I've never understood."

Reed remembered packing his kitchen up in Chicago and coming face-to-face with the worst reminder that he'd had Jordan and then lost him–one of his beloved French presses.

"Yeah, she's not weird at all. Not like some people who drink boiling hot coffee when it's a hundred degrees outside."

Jordan's disgruntled expression melted away into a wide smile and he laughed. "Don't buy her a gift card. I've seen her admiring this very fancy iced coffee tumbler during more than one coffee break." He reached around Reed, barely brushing his shoulder, and grabbed it.

Reed told himself the reason he flinched was because he hadn't had someone invade his personal space in awhile, but it was a lie. It was Jordan. Only Jordan. Even the most casual brush of his hand across the cotton of the t-shirt he wore was enough to send shivers down his spine.

Reed shook it off and took the tumbler from Jordan. "What else?"

Laughing, Jordan waved at the line in front of the register. "More gifting advice requires payment. Coffee for me, iced tea for you."

It felt like such a slippery slope; buying Jordan coffee ostensibly so he could pump him for info on Jemma's preferences, when in reality he was doing it because he'd missed doing it.

Missed the way Jordan's eyes lit up with his first sip of strong, hot caffeine. Missed the way he cradled the cup in his hands. Missed the way he'd often faintly smelled like fresh-roasted coffee beans.

Reed knew he was a pathetic pining idiot, but missing the aroma of roasting coffee beans might be the worst evidence yet.

"Did you talk to Quentin about the episode he suggested?" Reed asked while they stood in line. Talking about work was safe, even if the episode in question was the Italian dinner party double episode where Reed and Jordan were going to be guests.

"He might have mentioned it." Jordan's voice was carefully neutral.

"I should have told him that his already transparent matchmaking schemes were becoming increasingly transparent. Instead all I said was it was a good idea."

Reed had a feeling his statement might break Jordan's neutrality, and like clockwork, his face went bright red. "Right. Well. You're not stupid."

"It's a good idea," Reed repeated. "Or else I might have said that."

"Does it bother you?" Jordan asked, wincing a little.

Reed had had a few days to think about the last few schemes–the movie night, the Italian dinner party episode–and he'd come to the conclusion that no, they didn't bother him. But the question was whether to be honest with Jordan about it. He hadn't decided yet what to do with Jordan, if there was even anything *to* do with him, and he didn't want to give Jordan the wrong impression.

But in the end, he couldn't lie; he could only deflect. "Does it bother *you*?" Reed asked.

A glimmer of a smile showed through on Jordan's face, but instead of answering, he stepped forward to order. Reed hoped the timely interruption might have saved both of them from a question he wasn't sure they wanted answered yet.

But after ordering, instead of letting the subject drop, Jordan picked it right back up. "I asked you first," he insisted impudently, shooting Reed a quick grin.

"Well," Reed hesitated. "It doesn't bother me. I don't know what to do with it half the time, and I'm sure I'm awkward as hell. But I don't hate it."

Jordan took a moment, clearly thoughtfully considering this answer. "I don't hate it either," he finally announced. "And I think you're adorable when you're awkward."

Reed wanted to groan in frustration. Half the time it felt like Jordan seemed perfectly fine with the status quo, and the other half of the time he said these outrageous statements that thoroughly fucked with Reed's sanity.

Instead of going a step further and demanding what that meant exactly, Reed fell back on a comfortable standard–he changed the subject. Which, considering Jordan's knowing smile, he understood all too well. "You got your coffee. Now tell me what else Jemma might like."

Jordan changed the subject right back. "What have you gotten for Secret Santa?"

Reed barely avoided grinding his teeth in frustration. "I don't see why it matters." He was still halfway convinced his Secret Santa was Jordan, and he wasn't going to give him the satisfaction of admitting how thoughtful and perfect his first gift had been.

Or how much Reed really wanted it to be from Jordan.

"I'm just curious. Lots of people base their gifting on what they get themselves." It was total bullshit, they both knew it, and Reed debated calling him on it. Jordan sat back in one of the rickety chairs and smiled.

"I got something great, which is why I want to give Jemma something great. Okay?"

"I'm glad," was all Jordan said smoothly. Sometimes Reed didn't know whether he wanted to spank him or kiss him. Or both. At the same time.

Dragging his mind back up from the gutter, Reed refocused. "Ideas for Jemma? Please?"

"She really likes pedicures from the nail place down the street. Also massages. Do the hot stone one, that's her favorite. Also she's a godawful cook so maybe a coupon for a free cooking lesson when she gets back from her honeymoon wouldn't go amiss. Her fiancé certainly wouldn't mind the gesture."

Reed pulled his phone from his pocket and made notes for himself while Jordan waited patiently.

"You're actually close," Reed said. "I didn't really believe Landon when he told me you were, but it turns out some things aren't a matchmaking ploy."

Jordan laughed. "About one in ten right now, give or take."

"I'll keep that in mind," Reed grumbled. He'd figured as much, but it was still annoying. Except when it threatened to work and it suddenly wasn't.

"I can't believe your Secret Santa has only given you one gift," Jordan said casually. "What a crappy Secret Santa you've got."

"Maybe they're aiming for quality over quantity," Reed said. He didn't exactly know why he felt compelled to defend his Secret Santa to Jordan—especially if his Secret Santa *was* Jordan.

"Well, you'll have to let me know if they get you something awesome," Jordan said, rising to his feet. "I've got a meeting in five, but thanks for the coffee."

It was only at that moment that Reed realized that Jordan had managed to maneuver him into what might be considered a half-date.

"Thanks for the advice," Reed said. He felt tongue-tied and stupid, which had almost stopped happening around Jordan by the time they'd broken up, and he'd feel even dumber if he followed him to the elevator. So even though he had no reason to stay, he sat at the rickety table and drank his iced tea until Jordan had disappeared from view.

He timed three minutes by his phone, then got to his feet and took the elevator back upstairs. When he walked into his office, and saw what was sitting on his desk, he swore.

It was a near replica to the tumbler Reed had just bought for Jemma. Except this one was for iced tea, not coffee. His drink of choice. And also in the simply but elegantly put together gift bag was a membership to a six month "tea of the month" club.

Nobody else but Jordan would know that Reed preferred iced tea in the summer, hot tea in the winter.

Nobody else would have the nerve to disparage his Secret Santa's gifting abilities and then compliment his own gift a second later.

Reed didn't know whether to stomp down the hall to Jordan's cubicle and tell him he *knew* or whether to sit and let the game play out the way fate–or Landon–had designed it.

He sat down and looked again at the tumbler. Upon further inspection, it was even nicer than the one he'd gotten for Jemma, with a freezable insert for the middle of the container, to keep whatever liquid it contained cold. And it was the precise shade of leafy green that Reed had told Jordan once was his favorite.

What Reed had never told him was that it was the exact shade of Jordan's eyes.

Regret still felt like a useless emotion to Reed, except that now he was filled with it. Especially over something as stupid as not telling Jordan that his favorite color of green had always been the color of his eyes.

He was one hundred percent *a* pathetically pining idiot. The only question remained, what was he going to do about it?

Jordan tapped a pen impatiently on the desk.

Having already had a number of meetings with Landon and Quentin, Jordan knew how they could be. They didn't fight per se, but they bickered—well, *Landon* bickered, and Quentin rarely rose to his bait—and flirted and said about a hundred inappropriate things for every ten appropriate ones.

But this was supposed to be a meeting about *Dream Team*, not Jordan's love life, and he'd already endured Landon interrogating him frontwards, backwards, and then sideways about Reed.

"Does he think you're his Secret Santa?" Landon asked again, for probably the fourth time. Like Jordan's non-committal answer the first three times hadn't even happened.

"He's smart, he'll figure it out," Jordan said, which he hoped was true. He'd never expected to be able to fool Reed through the whole game. Reed was brand new to *Five Points* and nobody knew him that well–except for Jordan. And Jordan fully intended to use everything he'd gleaned from all those months of dating to his advantage.

"He'd better," Landon sniffed.

Jordan knew part of Landon's "master plan" revolved around Reed figuring out and appreciating that the gifts he was receiving were from Jordan. But frankly, he'd spent almost no time paying attention to most of Landon's schemes.

"Let's talk about the dinner party episode," Jordan said, because if he couldn't get Landon off the Reed topic today, he might as well use it.

"I think Quen has the menu set now," Landon said.

"I'm still trying to decide between marinated burrata and roasted red pepper bruschetta as the starter," Quentin said.

Jordan appreciated food because it tasted good when he put it in his mouth. Otherwise, he was a complete novice in the kitchen. Maybe not as bad as Landon, but then they'd both done the smart thing and grabbed men who were brilliant chefs.

Of course, Landon had managed to hold onto his. Jordan, not so much.

Some days it was really fucking hard not to be bitter. After semi-tricking Reed into having a drink with him at the Starbucks downstairs–and missing him so much it was hard to breathe–today was one of those days. It made sitting through this meeting where Landon couldn't seem to stop talking about Reed an exercise in both patience and pain management.

"What else is on the menu?" Jordan asked.

"Bolognese for the main. I want to make fresh pasta too," Quentin said, "and Reed suggested tiramisu for the dessert."

Jordan was more than a little surprised. One of his favorite desserts? Reed might as well have suggested one of his famous crème brûlée variations, like the one they'd shared during their first night together.

"That's a lot to cover, even in a double episode," Jordan said dubiously.

"We can do it," Landon said confidently. "If anyone can figure it out, it's you and Reed."

There isn't a me and Reed anymore, Jordan wanted to say, but he bit his tongue. The problem was that once he'd allowed Landon–and to a lesser extent, his boyfriend–to set themselves on this course, it was hard to push them off of it, even when Jordan didn't think he needed the help.

Reed, while still wary, was thawing. Very slowly, but then Jordan couldn't expect anything more. He'd fucked up by not coming right after Reed and telling him explicitly how important he was. And then he'd fucked up even more by not doing it every day after that.

Jordan cleared his throat. "We'll see what we can do. If there was one thing you'd feel okay leaving out, what would it be?"

"I guess we could use dried pasta," Quentin said dubiously.

"Like the rest of the world does," Landon inserted.

Quentin shot him a frustrated look. "What," Landon retorted. "Not everyone has three hours to spend making dinner. *You* don't even have three hours to spend making dinner anymore."

"Right," Jordan said. He was not in the mood for Landon and Quentin's bickering today. "We can maybe go with a high-low theme. How to dress up basics like store-bought mozzarella or roasted red peppers or dried pasta and make them elegant enough for a party."

Quentin did not look convinced. Which didn't necessarily mean it was the end of the idea; instead, Jordan knew he'd need to roll out more convincing arguments. Quentin usually had strong concepts, but he was also reasonable.

Jordan knew he was taking on a lot more of the producer's responsibility for *Dream Team*, and he and Nick had talked that over right before Reed had come on board. Nick had expressed concern that he and Reed could work together harmoniously. Jordan had reassured him that it wouldn't be an issue. What he'd known was that Reed would naturally be focused on the culinary side and the rest of the production decisions would feel overwhelming to him, at least at first. Jordan was doing him a favor taking those off his plate.

Someday, when things were marginally less awkward, they'd talk about the way they divided the decisions on shows like *Dream Team* but for now, Jordan figured that if it wasn't broken, why fix it? The Italian dinner party episode, he'd decided, would be the ultimate proof if their system was working in the short term.

"So, as guests on the show," Jordan said, "have you thought about what our role might be?"

He knew very well that Landon and Quentin had spent zero time considering what their roles might be. They'd only struck upon it as a great matchmaking scheme, had probably patted themselves on the back for their brilliance, and that had been the end of it.

Their blank looks only confirmed what Jordan already suspected.

"Right," Jordan said. He sat back in his chair and waited, staring at the pair in front of him with an expectant expression.

Landon was the first to recover. "What do you mean, *role*?"

"Are we cooking? Talking? Eating? Standing there like cardboard cutouts?"

Landon went pale underneath his tan.

"Oh, yeah, well, of course you're talking. And eating."

"And cooking? We're going to look really stupid standing there doing nothing," Jordan retorted.

"Or really cute together," Landon muttered.

"What was that, pop star?" Jordan asked sweetly.

"Nothing." Landon plastered on one of his brightest smiles. The one he generally reserved for interviewers he didn't like.

"They might help cook, babe," Quen said to Landon, who just shrugged. For Landon, the cooking part of *Dream Team* ranked considerably lower than pretty much everything else.

"If you want to cook all these things in forty minutes," Jordan interrupted before Landon could respond, "you might want our help."

"Reed *is* a great chef," Landon mused. As if he actually cared. As if they were actually cooking any of the recipes. Jordan knew Landon still hadn't gotten accustomed to the fact that they didn't really cook any of the food during the show. As he put it, they played with fake food for eight minutes and spent twelve shamelessly flirting.

Since Jordan scripted most of the shameless flirting, he couldn't exactly disagree.

"Why don't you start thinking about how you'd like to divide up the workload between you and Landon and me and Reed?" Jordan suggested.

"Are you going to be coordinating with Reed about breaking down the recipes into steps?" Landon asked innocently. As if Landon didn't have a single ulterior motive in getting them to work together.

"Sure," Jordan said, because it was easier to agree than to go into all the reasons why he wanted to say no. Or why he didn't really want to say no at all.

"Perfect, now what else is on the agenda?" Landon asked. From the self-satisfied edge to his voice, Jordan had a feeling Landon had already fixed Jordan and Reed in his mind. Jordan wished he knew how to fix them.

It was hard for Jordan to keep the eye roll to himself but he managed it. "Only the rest of the ten episodes we're doing this season."

Landon let out an exaggerated groan. "Nick and Colin's annual holiday barbecue is tonight. I can't stay too late. I have to go home and pick out an outfit."

"Yeah, he's convinced a lot of celebrities will be there," Quentin chimed in, good-naturedly rolling his eyes at his boyfriend. "When it's actually mostly *Five Points* staff. It's not like the barbecues they used to host in Miami when Colin invited his whole team."

"Some of us have a reputation to maintain," Landon sniffed.

"Do you know if Reed is going?" Jordan asked.

"Are you asking," Landon questioned, "because if he's going, you're going to avoid it, or are you asking because you want to make sure you're both going?"

"Maybe he's just asking," Quentin pointed out before Jordan could answer. The truth was, Jordan wasn't entirely sure why he wanted to know.

Did he want to see Reed? Of course he did. He always wanted to see Reed, even when they'd been at their worst.

"I'm not going to avoid him," Jordan said, which was as honest as he cared to be.

"He's softening towards you," Landon insisted. "I know he is."

"The sooner we can work through the next ten episodes," Jordan said, "the sooner you're free to go get ready for the barbecue."

It wasn't quite enough motivation to keep Landon entirely focused, but it helped.

Jordan stood in his walk-in closet and tried to decide what to wear to the barbecue.

"I'm becoming Landon," he announced to a rack full of button-up shirts, who wisely didn't have a response.

He moved on from the button-ups onto another rack full of polo shirts. He flipped through them, discarding everything that was from his NFL days when it felt like everything he wore had to have a logo on it. He stopped on a bright blue shirt. He couldn't be completely sure, but something made him believe that he'd worn this one of the times he'd shown up at Garnet, alone, hoping he'd be able to capture the chef's attention.

Maybe it was even from the visit when he'd finally done it, and they'd shared dessert and the best first kiss he'd ever had.

For a long time, he'd hoped it was the last first kiss he'd ever experience. The hope had taken a beating over the last year, but as he pulled the shirt from the hanger, it felt new and fresh again.

After dressing, he grabbed his keys and hesitated.

He dialed Reed's number before he could overthink it. He was just being helpful; a *gentleman*, which is what his mom had always raised him to be. Jordan had always believed that it applied whether he dated men or women, and he still believed that, even though he'd settled pretty certainly on the former.

Reed picked up on the third ring. "Hey," Jordan said breathlessly. "I wondered if you wanted a ride to Colin and Nick's."

Reed was quiet for a long moment. Jordan's heart thudded in his chest. He'd only meant to offer a ride to the party–or had he?

"I was just about to call a cab," Reed said. "So yeah, that would be great."

Jordan felt breathless with the possibilities. "I'll be there in a few to pick you up."

He felt even more breathless when he pulled into the parking lot of Reed's complex, and Reed opened the passenger door. He was wearing all black, which made his eyes darker, and only seemed to emphasize the incredible body he had.

Jordan wanted to turn the car off and go upstairs. Wanted to strip off every offending piece of clothing with his teeth. Reed was gorgeous all the time, but he was extraordinary naked, like a piece of priceless art. The only difference was that Jordan would have paid any price, but he'd long learned that Reed, like anything really worth having, couldn't be bought.

"Do I look okay?" Reed asked, the thread of worry in his voice betraying the social anxiety Jordan knew he battled.

"You look great." Jordan briefly considered dragging Reed's hand over to his lap and showing him just how fantastic he thought Reed looked, but he'd made the wrong decision that first night by suggesting they hook up. He'd been trying since then to prove that he wasn't just around because he wanted casual sex.

Jordan was pulling out of the lot when Reed reached over and brushed a hand over Jordan's shoulder. It was a light touch, but that was all Reed had ever needed to make Jordan's heart race. "This looks familiar," Reed said.

"I might have worn it to Garnet, when we first met," Jordan admitted.

He chanced a look over in Reed's direction. In the sunset light, he looked contemplative, but also pleased. Jordan decided he'd gotten the right idea.

Reed let Jordan drive the first few minutes in silence, but then spoke up. "Have you ever been to Nick and Colin's house? I hear it's insane."

"Yeah, I have. The property is definitely insane. I know you haven't been around Colin much, but he's not really one for excess. The house is simple. The view is . . . not."

"When Nick invited me, he said most of *Five Points* was coming," Reed said, which someone who didn't know him as well as Jordan did might have misunderstood. Jordan knew Reed didn't like crowds, or big parties. They made him nervous. He didn't always know what to say when confronted with a bunch of strangers.

"Yeah, a lot of work will be there. And some of Colin's friends, ex-teammates of mine, actually," Jordan said. "If you want to stick close . . ."

Jordan still wasn't sure how he was going to end that question, but Reed nodded emphatically anyway. That was how they'd always done parties. With Jordan next to him, smoothing the way, Reed hadn't felt as awkward or uncomfortable.

"If it isn't a problem," Reed said. He shifted a little in the leather seat, and Jordan took advantage of a stoplight to glance over at him.

"It's never a problem," Jordan answered honestly. He wanted to tell Reed that he wasn't just doing it to help Reed out either; that his favorite place to be was always at Reed's side. But he didn't want to say it and make Reed even more uncomfortable. "Plus," he added, "Landon and Quen will be there. Rory and Kimber. I know you aren't as familiar with Jemma or her fiancé, but they'll be there too. You can ask her if she liked her Secret Santa gift."

Reed laughed. "You don't think that sort of defeats the secret portion of the game?"

"To be honest, I think most of the secrets are rather badly kept by this point," he said. He wondered if now would be the moment that Reed chose to confront him about his own gifts, which, if Reed was paying attention at all, would have had to come from him.

But he stayed quiet, and there wasn't another opportunity, because that was when Jordan pulled the car onto the long, winding driveway that led to Nick and Colin's house.

The valet opened the door for him, and Jordan stepped out, handing the other man his keys. Turning, he met Reed's eyes across the top of the car.

"You ready?" Jordan asked.

Reed nodded, but still looked apprehensive. "Let's go get a drink," Jordan suggested, "and then we'll make the rounds."

Light and sound was spilling out the front door and Jordan could tell from the number of cars, a lot of people had already arrived. Without thinking, Jordan reached out his hand for Reed to take. They'd always done it at parties, giving Reed something to ground him. Reed's eyes flew to Jordan's, and he hesitated a moment before reaching out and taking it.

Reed's big, warm palm settling in his felt like coming home. Jordan had never been happier than when he was with Reed, and nothing had changed.

When they walked in the house, Nick and Colin were in the entry, greeting guests. Jordan could see both of them take in their linked hands, but they didn't say anything, just told them to make themselves at home and pointed the way to the bar.

The bar was at the back of the house. As they crossed the warm dark wood floors, Jordan could barely look away from Reed as the man next to him took in the stark simplicity of the style that seemed to define Colin and Nick as a couple. Large open spaces. Huge, floor-to-ceiling windows highlighting the incredible view of the ocean. Simple furniture. No clutter anywhere.

"Their other house is just like this, except it's on a private island with its own beach," Jordan murmured to Reed as they made their way over to the bar.

"Of course it is," Reed said wryly after he'd ordered their beers. "Why am I not surprised?"

"Most rich people have *terrible* taste," Jordan said. They paused at the entrance to the large yard, people milling around in clumps near two long draped tables full of food.

"Do you sometimes hate them?" Reed asked as they made their way over to the food. "Not hate, but you know, be generally soul-curdlingly jealous of their perfect life?"

Jordan laughed and dropped Reed's hand so he could pick up a plate. And like sixteen months hadn't passed, he felt Reed's hand settle on the small of his back. It was a light touch, but it was there. Jordan nearly dropped the plate and dragged Reed off to the nearest dark corner of the yard. He might have done it too, if not for how Reed had reacted that first night, and at the gym. He clearly had not been ready even a f As they finished filling their plates and went to sit down on a natural rock bench to eat, a particular question burned in Jordan's head. ew days ago. He probably wasn't ready now.

"Yeah," Jordan answered honestly. "I think it would be unusual not to feel that way about them once in awhile. But they're nice enough that it's hard to keep feeling that way."

As they finished filling their plates and went to sit down on a natural rock bench to eat, a particular question burned in Jordan's head. "What would you have done if I hadn't called you?" he asked.

Reed considered this for a long moment. "I was hoping you'd call," he admitted. "Otherwise, I probably would have hid in the corner after finally getting up the balls to walk inside. This is a pretty incredible house."

"I should have remembered how you were about parties," Jordan admitted. "I mean, I knew, but I didn't think you'd want…" He didn't want to say *me*, but it hung between them anyway, unsaid.

"Funny," Reed said, and he was smiling, "I thought the same thing."

Jordan pushed away the pulse of guilt that Reed would ever feel unwanted by him. It was easy enough to assume that he'd felt that way when he'd left LA and Jordan hadn't ever talked to him again.

"You shouldn't," Jordan said, leaning in until their foreheads nearly touched. He'd forgotten how Reed's eyes always fluttered closed, his eyelashes so delicate despite the muscular solidness of his body. "I never want you to think that." He wanted to dip his head even closer until they kissed, hot mustard on his breath and all these people be damned, but of course Landon chose that particular moment to interrupt. Jordan was beginning to think there was some sort of conspiracy to prevent him and Reed from getting too close. First Quen, now Landon. *Ugh.*

"You guys are here!" Landon exclaimed loudly, Quentin trailing behind him carrying two drinks. "Together!"

"Yes," Jordan retorted dryly as Reed moved back a few precious inches. Jordan wanted to reach over and pull him right back. "Together."

Next to him, Reed barely managed to muffle a laugh.

"What do you think of the house?" Landon asked.

"Almost makes me want to become a quarterback in the NFL," Reed said.

Landon shot Jordan a very un-subtle look. Jordan wasn't entirely sure what the purpose was, but he had a feeling it was something like, *this is your opening, get on that right now.* Except that Jordan knew his old job had never helped his chances with Reed; in the end, it had been partly to blame for why they'd fallen apart.

Landon also didn't know that Jordan had been doing very well for himself before he'd been interrupted again.

"I think Rory is over there," Quentin said, gently reaching in and tugging on Landon's arm. "We'll see you guys around." As they turned to leave, Quen gave Jordan a quick, reassuring nod.

"I remember the first time I met Landon," Reed said when the pair was out of earshot. "I'd never met Quentin either, but I remember thinking Landon fulfilled all my prior expectations, but he was still very different from what I'd anticipated."

Jordan remembered the first time he'd met Landon, and that he'd not been surprised at all. But then, he'd binge-watched *Kitchen Wars* about a hundred times at that point and he'd felt like he'd already known the man even though they'd never officially met.

"How so?" he asked Reed. Reed didn't often give his opinions on things that weren't related to food. He tended to keep those to himself, but Jordan always wanted to know what he was thinking.

"He's in everyone's business. He's persistent and he never stops talking. But he's genuine, too. He means well, every single time. It surprised me how selfless he is."

It amazed Jordan that after he'd known this man for over two years, Reed still managed to surprise him. "I've never thought of Landon as particularly selfless before," Jordan admitted.

Reed gestured with his beer bottle. "But now that I've said it, you can't stop."

"I'm going to have to be nicer to him in meetings now, thanks to you," Jordan grumbled.

"Hey, you're the one who saved *Dream Team*. Don't tell me you didn't know what you were getting into," Reed teased, nudging Jordan's shoulder with his own.

"I really did," Jordan said. "And it wasn't just for them, either." He took a deep breath, really wondering if he should be this honest, but knowing deep down that he'd spent too much time not telling Reed the truth. "I did it because it felt like the last connection, no matter how slim, I had to you."

Reed looked surprised.

"I know, I should have said something a long time ago," Jordan continued softly. "I'm sorry I didn't."

"Maybe . . . maybe it was good you didn't. We both messed up. I shouldn't have left. And I shouldn't have assumed long distance would end us."

"This probably isn't the right place to talk about this . . ." Jordan said, because his heart was in his throat. He could only hope that the rest of the party could see they were buried in an important, sixteen-months-coming discussion, and would leave them alone.

Landon included. "But maybe you'd want to look around the rest of the grounds?"

Reed grinned, and it was like the sun breaking over the clouds. "Sure. And I do want to talk just . . . not here. Not right now. But soon."

Jordan got to his feet and dusted off his pants. He held out a hand to Reed. "Soon," he agreed. "But not tonight."

Hand in hand, Jordan took Reed to the edge of the property, where people were scarce. The last remnants of the sun were about to finish setting over the Pacific, and they bathed everything they touched with an unearthly golden light. Jordan thought he saw the same thing he was feeling reflected back in Reed's eyes, and he couldn't hold back anymore.

"I missed you so much," Jordan confessed. To his surprise, Reed reacted to Jordan's words by wrapping his arms around his waist and pulling him closer.

"Missed you too," Reed murmured into the crook of Jordan's neck. He felt the puff of Reed's warm breath on his skin and shivered. "Saw a lot of places. Amazing places. Not so amazing without you."

Jordan slipped a hand up Reed's muscular back, to the curve of the back of his neck. Tugged him back because he wanted to see his face. The ghosts haunting him weren't completely gone but he looked lighter than Jordan had seen since he'd come back. "If you don't want . . . this," he said hesitatingly, resting his forehead against Reed's. He couldn't do this and not have it mean something.

But Reed had already said it meant something. He'd said so the first night.

The question was if it would mean everything. Jordan knew he was going to have to wait for that particular answer until Reed was ready to give it. Reed, who was so careful and methodical about everything, had made that very clear.

There were a lot of wonderful things about their first kiss. Jordan still remembered it fondly. When Reed kissed him this time, Jordan wasn't just intrigued and insatiably curious about this chef he'd just met. This time, he knew he loved Reed. Knew this man was something special, something unforgettable. And he knew he wasn't letting him go again.

Reed's tongue and his hands wandered almost at precisely the same moment. The kiss, sweet and a little innocent up until that moment, flamed hotter almost instantly. Jordan tried hard not to groan into Reed's mouth as his fingers tugged his shirt out of his pants and slipped underneath, Reed touching his skin for the first time in way too long. He could feel Reed's hard-on against his thigh, hot and solid and far too tempting.

Jordan ended the kiss, panting a little embarrassingly. It had been a long time, which was probably something he should tell Reed.

Except that Reed spoke first. "We could have saved a lot of trouble if you'd just said the first night that you didn't want to only screw around." He was smiling.

"You assumed I just wanted to screw around," Jordan retorted, except that he had sort of implied it was just casual. Mostly because he was too terrified to imply the truth, which was that he was still head over heels for this man.

Reed was quiet for a long moment. "I think," he finally said, "it was hard for me to believe you wanted to be with me, when you could have anyone you wanted. That's never been your fault, but when things fell apart, I let it happen because deep down, I expected it. I think that's why I ran."

"Then kept running." Jordan rubbed a reassuring hand up and down Reed's back. He didn't understand Reed's insecurities but he *got* them. "I'm sorry I didn't run after you."

Jordan swore he could feel Reed smile against his shoulder. "I thought we weren't supposed to be talking," he said.

"You started it," Jordan teased back. He pulled back, so he could look directly at Reed when he asked. It had always surprised him that Reed was shorter than him; he always seemed larger than life. "You wanna head back to my place and not talk for awhile?"

"I do," Reed said, and he sounded genuinely tempted. "But I'm not sure I'm ready for that yet."

Jordan couldn't pretend he wasn't disappointed. "Can I at least claim this was a date?" he asked hopefully.

Reed's dark eyes glowed from the light of the torches set around the backyard. "If this is a date, does that mean you'll get me a drink?"

"I'll do anything you want me to do," Jordan said. It might have been too honest, but he'd spent far too long not telling the truth. Maybe he was making up for lost time.

"Well, we've already kissed," Reed said, "and I fully intend to kiss you again. So it's definitely a date."

Chapter Six

REED DID WHAT REED always did when he felt uncertain about any-thing in his personal life—he retreated to the kitchen. This time to the *Five Points* kitchens, since the Garnet kitchen was long lost.

Are we dating, again? Reed questioned as he set up his *mise en place*. The problem was he didn't know. They still hadn't cleared all the air, and the hurt and guilt he'd carried for so long hadn't faded completely, even though it was growing dimmer by the day.

Each ingredient was perfectly ordered on the kitchen counter for when he'd need it next. Consulting the printed recipe Quentin had given him, he ran through the list of steps one last time before he began. Normally, he didn't enjoy cooking from recipes, but he needed to verify for himself that the recipes *Dream Team* would be filming were as flawless as they could be before he gave his final approval.

Quentin had decided to make tiramisu for the Italian dinner party Reed was still trying to convince Nick to okay. Reed couldn't believe he was fighting for something so much when it was all some horribly transparent scheme to throw Jordan and him together again.

But Reed had made peace with the idea in the days after the barbecue at Colin and Nick's house. He and Jordan still needed to talk, but the real question wasn't what Reed wanted to say, but when he should say it.

Like Reed's thoughts had summoned him, the door to the kitchens opened, and Jordan stuck his head inside.

"Oh, I was looking for Quentin. I didn't realize you were still around."

Despite working at the same company, Reed had realized that Jordan never pushed his presence onto Reed. Other people did—Landon, in particular—but never Jordan. He always asked. He always held back. He always waited until Reed expressed an opinion about his presence, and then he followed it to the letter.

He didn't presume now, hesitating in the doorway, unsure whether to stay or go.

Reed had been trying to figure out a casual way to approach Jordan so they could talk. He knew he could call him up and suggest they have dinner—but he wasn't happy with that plan either, because he knew the chances were they'd end up in bed right away. It was a miracle they hadn't after the gym or after the barbecue. Certain parts of Reed were very ready for that to happen, but his heart wasn't. His head wasn't. And he wasn't prepared to fuck their relationship up again, this time before it even begun.

But Reed discovered that this impromptu moment was perfect. He'd be in the kitchen, his comfort zone, and from the first moment they'd met, Jordan had always had a soft spot for Chef Reed.

"I was just about to run through Quentin's tiramisu recipe, for the Italian dinner party episode. You could help me," he suggested.

If Reed had announced he was going to become a football player, Jordan couldn't have looked more surprised. "Really?" he asked skeptically.

"It's one of your favorite desserts," Reed said. "You might as well learn how to make it. If Quentin's recipe is any good, that is."

Jordan slipped into the kitchen, the door closing behind him. He wandered over to where Reed was prepping. Standing close enough to see but just far enough away that he wasn't anywhere near Reed's personal space. Reed got that; it was probably born out of self-preservation more than anything else. He could still feel the soft slide of Jordan's skin under his fingertips. "Better not let Landon hear you say that," he said.

"If he finds out, I'll know exactly who told him."

Jordan raised an eyebrow. "A lot more cutthroat than I remember."

"I'm the boss now, got to draw the line somewhere." Reed tried to joke about it, but he was all too aware how flat his voice sounded.

"You were the boss at Garnet," Jordan pointed out, leaning against the opposite counter. Reed glanced back and forced his mind not to start reminiscing about their first kiss. While a good way to spend an hour, it wouldn't get this tiramisu made.

"It's not the same," Reed admitted. "I hand-picked all those people. I knew most of them before they ever worked for me. These are all strangers, and they're looking to me to lead them."

"Everyone at Garnet would've walked across fire for you. You're right, it's not the same. But I know you'll figure it out and be great. You never understand how easy it is for you to win people over. You aren't trying, but they're on your side anyway."

Reed didn't know what to say to that–it pricked at the insecurities he'd held onto for so long–so he picked up an egg. "Would you read me the recipe, a line at a time? It'll help things go faster. I know I need to separate the eggs first. Anything else?"

Jordan reached over, slipping for the first time into Reed's personal space, and picked up the recipe. "Did you already brew the espresso?"

Nodding, Reed cracked an egg with a single fluid motion, separating out the white from the yolk using the broken shell. "Then you're all good," Jordan said. "I can't believe how easy you make that look."

Reed glanced over at the other man. "You've separated eggs?" "This trainer wanted me only eating egg whites for awhile. It was torture."

"The training or the separating?" Reed made quick work of the remaining eggs. Not a speck of white showing in the sunny yellow yolks.

Jordan rolled his eyes. "The separating. The training wasn't all that great either. He was a guy I met after you left LA. Didn't like him much."

"You didn't like him?" This fact divided Reed's attention from the eggs he was whisking with sugar. "You like everybody."

"He was a self-important prick," Jordan grumbled.

"Did the team hire him?" It was a guess, but Reed knew something drastic—more than one drastic somethings, if he was being honest—would have had to have occurred for Jordan to leave football. He hadn't loved playing for his new team, but he'd still loved the game and had been determined to finish out his contract.

"Yeah," Jordan said.

"That why you retired early?"

Jordan laughed and it was vaguely bitter. "Don't pull any punches or anything."

Reed set the whisk in the bowl and lifted his arms in mock surrender. "I'm curious, okay? Because when I left, you weren't necessarily happy, but you meant to finish your contract out. And I wondered what could have changed your mind."

"A lot of things," Jordan said. His arms were folded across his chest and he didn't look mad, but he didn't look very happy either. "So we're going to talk, then?"

Reed flushed as he picked the whisk back up. "We said we would."

"I was letting you decide when and where," Jordan said, which Reed had already figured out. Ever since the barbecue, Jordan had been giving him space.

"You knew I was coming to LA. I was surprised. I've needed more time to . . . process." Reed paused. "Next?"

"Add the mascarpone cheese, beat until combined."

Reed glanced at the whisk in his hand. "I'm not sure this is going to do the trick," he said. "Maybe we should switch to the mixer."

"And deprive me of a show?" Jordan teased. "I used to lie in bed and watch you make us omelets in the morning. You'd be shirtless and I'd love to watch you beat the eggs. Your biceps were gorgeous."

"I never understand why you don't tell me these things *at the time*," Reed grumbled, pulling out the hand mixer from a cabinet.

"I don't know," Jordan confessed. "It does seem stupid, doesn't it? I do think them, but they just never make it to my mouth. Maybe I should work on that."

Reed shot him a sideways glance. "Maybe you should."

"Which one is the mascarpone cheese?" Jordan asked. He was sorting through the *mise en place,* but out of the corner of his eye Reed could see that he was being particularly careful not to change the order of anything. Reed finished unwinding the mixer cord and started a hunt for where they had hid the outlets in this kitchen.

Like when Jordan had offered to stay with him during the barbecue, it warmed Reed's heart back up and made him want to believe that Jordan meant every word he said. "It's that stack of containers," Reed said, gesturing with the hand mixer. "Can you grab a spatula and get those scooped out into the bowl while I find the stupid outlet?"

"If you were attempting for authenticity," Jordan said, "you'd whip it by hand. Like a little Italian *nonna.*"

Reed opened and shut three cupboards. "I'm not Italian or a *nonna.*"

"Or little," Jordan said blandly. "My bad."

Reed gestured with the mixer, its metal whisks standing in for a middle finger. He sighed in defeat. "You know where the outlets are, don't you?"

Not even looking contrite, Jordan reached over and flipped open the outlet covers on the backsplash. "I can't believe I knew a kitchen thing you didn't," Jordan said.

"Someday," Reed said sternly as he plugged in the mixer, "you're going to get a good, hard spanking for that mouth of yours."

Reed realized a half-second too late what he'd just said and he glanced up at Jordan instinctively. Jordan's eyes met Reed's and for an electric half-second, Reed almost said *fuck it*, and bent Jordan over the nearest counter.

He'd always prided himself on better self-control than that, but something about Jordan eroded it like it didn't exist.

"Promise?" Jordan asked softly.

"Don't," Reed said, more harshly than he'd intended.

They were both quiet for a minute. Jordan finished scooping the mascarpone into the bowl and slid it over towards Reed.

"I'm sorry, I swore to myself I wouldn't try to seduce you," Jordan said.

Reed sighed. "You don't even have to try. I want to take your hand and go back to your place or my place or maybe even the most convenient back seat right now. But this is important to me. I cut and run before, because I was afraid. I avoided every part of the relationship that was hard, and didn't confront any of our issues straight on. I'm not going to do that again."

"Sex would be a distraction," Jordan said solemnly.

"Why don't you say that like you mean it?" Reed said, chuckling.

"Ugh, because I don't want to be noble," Jordan said. "I want you again."

"Maybe we need a distraction." Reed knew he did, at least. "Tell me the story about why you quit football."

Reed started beating the mascarpone with the egg yolks and the sugar, letting Jordan have a moment to think about his answer.

"I meant it when I said there wasn't a single reason," Jordan said. "It wasn't really about you. It sort of was though because at that point everything was about you. I was sad and, frankly, fucking depressed, and football didn't give me the boost it once had. It felt like work, not play." He paused, and glanced over at Reed. "Don't you laugh. Isn't that one of Reed Ryan's most famous sayings? 'Work is play and play is work'?"

Reed snorted. "Everything is work, at some point or another. Besides, work isn't always bad."

"Anyway," Jordan said. "I didn't like the new team. I didn't like the coach. The locker room was tense as hell. The trainer was a nightmare. And I missed you like crazy. When Nick and I were at lunch one day and he mentioned he was hiring new writers, I knew instantly what I wanted to do. Nick hadn't even meant to suggest I take the job. He was just giving me an update on what was going on with him and the company, and he was probably–no, he was definitely–shocked as fuck when I emailed him my resume and some writing samples that night."

Reed turned off the mixer and set it on the bowl. "I was in Rio when I stopped by an internet café and realized that you'd quit. I felt responsible."

Jordan came up behind him, wrapping his arms around his shoulders, resting his head against Reed's. "No, *no*, it wasn't your fault. It was everything, all at once. You know I never wanted to play forever."

"I know," Reed admitted. "But it felt like the worst kind of guilt, at the worst time, because I was already feeling so guilty for losing *Kitchen Wars*."

He turned and wrapped Jordan up in his arms. "I never apologized for that," he continued. "I know I shut down after we got eliminated. And you deserved better."

"Sweetheart," Jordan said, a thread of amusement in his voice. "You were never going to win *Kitchen Wars*. You're way too serious, and frankly, too good of a chef. I knew that before you even started. And yeah, long distance sucked. I didn't like it either. But I only would have spent the time in LA that I had to. We could've made things work between us. It wouldn't have been easy, but you were worth it."

The lump that had existed in Reed's throat since he'd heard his name called as the eliminated chef finally began to dissolve. "You didn't think I'd win?" he even managed to say in mock outrage.

"I knew you wouldn't. You're not dramatic enough. Maybe if Diego had been a little more like Landon." Jordan let go of Reed, but his hand didn't leave his back. Reed thought he could even breathe a little easier with Jordan touching him. Or maybe that was all the shit they'd built up and never discussed finally being broken up a little bit at a time, like a lake slowly unfreezing.

"If Diego had been like Landon," Reed said earnestly, "we wouldn't have made it as far as we did."

"That's probably true, but it sure would have been great television," Jordan agreed.

Reed rolled his eyes. "Can you get the ladyfingers for me? They all need to be dunked in that espresso, mixed in with a little dark rum." He frowned. "I usually use marsala wine, but I guess this is Quentin's modern take on tiramisu."

"You're not usually such a traditionalist. Maybe Quen's way is better. Don't knock it 'til you've tried it. These are the ladyfingers, right?" he asked pointing to a plastic package of cookies. "The thing I can't believe is that you're using store-bought cookies."

"That's *definitely* traditional," Reed said.

"There," Jordan pointed out as he poured the espresso into a shallow bowl and added a generous glug of rum, "you nearly had Landon's disdainful tone down pat right there. A few more months of education and maybe we can shove you back on television and the world will fall in love with you too."

"I don't want the world to love me," Reed grumbled. "Just you."

Jordan glanced up in surprise. "You know I do. You have to know I love you."

Reed cleared his throat. He wasn't sure Jordan had been ready to say that again. He wasn't sure he was ready to hear it. "I wondered for a long time."

"Still?" Jordan persisted, looking very intently in Reed's direction.

"No," Reed had to answer honestly. "Not anymore." He leaned over and kissed Jordan, the grip of Reed's hands on his hips his poor attempt to communicate how happy he was that everything between them hadn't been destroyed. But more importantly, that he wasn't letting Jordan go anytime soon. *Ever*, if he had his way.

They worked together to assemble the rest of the tiramisu, layers of mascarpone cream piled on top of the espresso-soaked ladyfingers. Reed dusted the top with dark chocolate cocoa powder and leaned back against the counter as Jordan carefully slid it into the fridge.

"Now what?" Jordan asked.

"It's late, but it needs a few hours to set," Reed admitted. "You want to grab some dinner?"

"Date number two?" Jordan asked hopefully.

Reed nodded hesitantly. He wanted to. They'd started clearing the air. But the memory of the hurt still lingered.

"I'm just trying to figure out where your head's at," Jordan admitted.

Reed glanced over at him, his own expression serious and earnest. "Believe me, when it's the right time, you'll know."

Jordan took him to his favorite burger place, and as they were finishing their shakes–Reed vanilla, Jordan chocolate–he said, "Do you like Christmas lights?"

Reed shot him an incredulous look. "What sort of person doesn't?" he asked. "Of course I like Christmas lights."

"There's some great ones right around the corner from here," Jordan admitted. "Which is kinda why I brought you over this way, if I'm being honest."

"The burger was pretty good too," Reed said. "Was that true? Is this your favorite burger place?"

It was Jordan's turn to be serious. "I'm not going to lie to you again. Or stay quiet if I know I should say something. That's lying by omission and I'm not doing it anymore."

There was an earnestness to Jordan now that Reed didn't remember from their time in Chicago. It was very clear that Jordan had spent at least part of the last sixteen months also thinking about what he wanted out of his life. He'd arranged it the way he knew it should be, without catering to what anyone else wanted or thought would be cool.

Reed knew there were lots of people who didn't get why he'd turned in his football cleats for a laptop. He'd seen the comments online, and even though he hoped that Jordan hadn't, he knew better.

This new Jordan he was just getting to know would have looked at the comments and it would only have made him more certain of the path he knew was right for him.

"Tell me the truth then," Reed asked as they stepped outside into the evening air. It was still balmy in LA, totally different from the arctic tundra it had been the winter they'd been together in Chicago. "Did I really get the job at *Five Points* because I was the most qualified or did I get the job because you wanted to see me again?"

Jordan chuckled ruefully. "I hate to break it to you, but it honestly was not my idea, even though that would have been sickeningly romantic. Of course I wanted to see you again. I wanted to call you. Text you. I just . . . didn't. Didn't know how I could after so long. When you ended up on Nick's radar for the job, and he asked me what I thought of working with you again, I really did think it could be the worst thing or the best thing that could happen to me."

"When I saw you at the taco stand," Reed said, reaching for his hand. He'd let Jordan buy his burger and shake, and now they were holding hands. *Definitely* date number two. "I was sure it was fate, and at first I thought fate was being an asshole."

"And now?" Jordan asked hopefully. He tugged his hand and they turned down one street, and then two blocks down, another.

"Now, I think you know where I stand," Reed teased back playfully. "The real question is, do you even know where you're taking us, Casanova?"

"I'm pretty sure it's around this next block," Jordan said. "It's sort of the best kept secret in West Hollywood."

"What is?" Reed asked, as they turned down yet another street with only sparse Christmas lights. Not exactly the winter wonderland he'd been promised.

"It's one street where every house decorates big-time for Christmas. And you can drive down, but it's so much better to walk."

"Everybody decorates?" Reed questioned skeptically.

"At first it was just a neighborhood thing they did, but then I think they wrote it into their bylaws," Jordan admitted.

"Ah, the romance of a contract," Reed said.

Jordan glanced down at him, eyes shining in the glow of the streetlamps as they walked past. Reed couldn't remember the last time he'd looked this happy or this content. They'd both been deliriously happy those first few months in Chicago, but even then it hadn't felt like this did. Reed realized that, the whole time, he'd been halfway dreading in the back of his mind that the shoe would drop and the fairy tale would all end.

And of course, it had.

"Here it is," Jordan said. Reed had wondered if they were approaching, because the number of people milling in the streets had increased, until a crowd was gathered near the stop sign at the end of a small street.

Reed gasped as they got closer, because the light emanating from the street was a glow that could probably be seen from space. Whatever was down this street was a *lot* of Christmas lights.

There seemed to be a line of people meandering their way down one sidewalk and up the next, so Reed and Jordan joined it. Reed glanced down at their hands, still intertwined together. "Is this okay?" he asked in a hushed tone.

When they'd been in Chicago together, they'd had to be aware that Jordan was a public figure and also hadn't told his adoring fans that he was gay. So holding hands, at least out on the street like this in front of dozens of people, hadn't been something they could do.

Reed hadn't particularly minded. In the scheme of things, it hadn't seemed like a big deal–at least nothing compared to being in a relationship with Reed. But he couldn't deny there was something very reassuring about being able to be in public this way, with no concern that holding hands would cause a publicity disaster.

Jordan just shrugged. "I'm not hiding," he said, not even bothering to muffle his own voice. "I figure everyone will figure out who I like soon enough."

"I guess you don't really need to make an announcement anymore," Reed said.

"Besides," Jordan said with a smirk, "I have a feeling that everyone that watches the Italian dinner party episode will figure it out pretty quickly."

"Are you scripting us too?" Reed asked. He was both excited and a little terrified that Jordan was scripting them the sort of flirtatious banter that was the bread and butter of Landon and Quentin's interactions on *Dream Team*.

"I'm putting together . . . we'll call them 'talking points.'"

"Jordan," Reed said seriously, "you are not thinking about coming out during Landon and Quen's dinner party episode. Tell me you're not."

But Jordan didn't say anything, and the twinkle in his eyes seemed to put even the sparkly Christmas lights to shame as they approached the first houses on the street.

Reed had never seen so many Christmas lights together in one location. It was magical, the different variations of light and pattern and color, even sound, at some houses.

"You really should tell Quen and Landon," Reed said. "It's their show."

"And they pulled a silly matchmaking scheme on it," Jordan said, clearly unconcerned. "It's okay. They'll get it when they see the script, but somehow I don't think it'll bother them."

Reed had a very good idea of why Landon and Quentin might gloss over Jordan's choosing to use their show as a vehicle for coming out. The answer could only include him, in some shape or form. "I'm assuming you've already cleared this with Nick, and Duncan."

"Yep," Jordan said, and glanced over at him with an impudent smile. "Now I'm consulting my other producer on the issue."

"Is that all I am to this conversation?" Reed asked.

"You know you're not," Jordan said. "We're waiting on you. Which, I might add, is perfectly fine. I'll wait as long as you want me to, as long as you don't go away again."

Reed squeezed his hand, his eyes more interested in the man next to him than the Star Wars display they were looking at. Even though this particular house had a life-size Darth Vader, complete with a halo of red lights. He wasn't sure if this one was his favorite, or the rainbow palm trees three houses back.

"It's weird that it's not really cold. Or snowing," Reed observed as they finished up the other side of the street. "I feel like it's not the holidays because it isn't snowing."

"I went to school here. I grew up here. I'm fucking thrilled it isn't snowing. Christmas shouldn't be full of weather-induced misery," Jordan said.

Reed wasn't entirely sure he disagreed with him, now that he thought about it.

"No snow shovels, no ice storms, no grocery store mobs, no icy wind blowing down your neck no matter how tightly you tie your scarf," Jordan recited, like this was a list he'd considered.

"You make a solid point," Reed admitted. "Not that you ever shoveled snow. You lived in a high rise with a concierge and a full-time handyman."

"Still," Jordan persisted. "We couldn't have done this in Chicago without halfway freezing to death. Or," he added under his breath, "probably running into a dozen fans who wanted to take selfies."

It felt a little selfish and almost disloyal, but Reed didn't miss the invasive fans either. He also liked that Jordan didn't care if anyone knew anymore. Holding hands, which wasn't something he'd ever thought he needed with Jordan, was unexpectedly nice.

"How about we wind up our date with some fantastic tiramisu?" Reed asked, as they walked back to the car.

"So you're admitting this is a date now?" Jordan asked. He sounded very pleased.

"We could never be just friends," Reed confessed. "Not us."

"Not us," Jordan agreed.

Back at the *Five Points* office, they dug into the cold tiramisu with spoons by the dim light over the sink. And later, when Reed pulled Jordan close to kiss him again, he tasted like coffee and rum and Reed didn't know how he'd ever lasted without him.

CHAPTER SEVEN

TWO YEARS EARLIER

Reed dealt with the inevitable nerves of going on a date with Jordan Christensen by pretending it wasn't going to happen.

It worked pretty well and kept him calm from their first kiss to the first text Jordan had sent him to finalizing the day and time and venue. It worked all the way up until Reed stood in front of his closet, panicking about what he should wear.

The truth was he didn't give a shit about which shirt he threw on, it was just an easy thing to obsess over instead of obsessing over the fact that Jordan was going to be here to pick him up in five minutes.

Maybe instead of avoidance, he should have gone his normally-obsessive route and rehearsed things he could say, questions he could ask Jordan. Read a bunch of unhelpful advice online that might convince him once and for all that dating wasn't for him. At least he would've been prepared, Reed thought darkly.

He was debating between black and dark gray for the t-shirt he was going to wear—they were going to a real casual place of a friend of Reed's, because Jordan needed discretion and Reed was happy enough that the whole world wouldn't be witnesses to this first date that he'd been fine with it—when he heard the *thump, thump, thump* of Jordan's knock on his front door.

"Shit," Reed said and grabbed the black t-shirt, and was just trying to get it over his head as he pulled the door open.

Later, Reed would realize that coming to the door mostly shirtless was a brilliant move, but in the moment itself, he hadn't planned anything. He'd just been unable to make a fucking decision which shirt to wear until it was too late.

"Uh," Jordan said, while Reed tugged the fabric down over his head. "Uh."

"Sorry," Reed said breathlessly. Apologetically. *Please don't let him think I'm a major dork, almost late even though he's five minutes early.*

Jordan just stood there in the doorway, his normal eloquence departing him for silence. Reed's fear doubled, and then tripled. Why were they standing here, staring at each other? If they'd already run out of things to say, he was fucked, and not even in the fun way.

The way he'd definitely, absolutely thought about with Jordan. This week even lifting at the gym hadn't been enough to settle the hormones that seemed determined to rage through him. He'd thought about Jordan every single time he'd masturbated, which was a significantly higher rate than usual.

At the time, that had felt like self-preservation, because Reed was going out of his mind with how much he wanted Jordan. Now, it felt like utter stupidity, because it was inevitable that all those dirty thoughts rose right to the surface now, and inevitably, they were all he could think about.

Jordan on his knees. Jordan bending Reed over the nearest convenient surface. Jordan's cock. The way his skin would taste under Reed's tongue.

"How do you even look like that?" When Jordan finally opened his mouth, it was the last thing Reed expected him to say.

It shouldn't have put Reed more at ease to know that Jordan was off-kilter, but it did. It washed his jitters away and made him look more closely at the other man. His fists were clenched at his sides, and there was a particularly hot gleam in his eyes. Reed knew it was wrong, but he couldn't help but take a quick peek at what was hiding behind Jordan's fly. Yeah, he was definitely turned on.

"Like what?"

"Like…" Jordan waved his arms around, "like you were sculpted by Michelangelo. Like you don't cook incredible food for a living and probably eat a lot of it yourself."

Reed suddenly understood. Not many people expected him to spend hours in the gym after every evening, working off the adrenaline high of a dinner service. He shrugged. "I go to the gym a lot."

Reed swore Jordan's eyes darkened. He took a step forward, and then another, until he was nearly crowding into Reed. The door shut behind him, and Reed felt so awkward. He wanted to kiss Jordan, to ignite what had been gathering between them since the moment they'd met, but he didn't want to presume. He wished he could just jump into things the way other people did, instead of obsessively considering every angle and every possible rejection.

"Someday," Jordan said, moving even closer, until Reed was nearly backed up against the wall next to the front door, "you're going to let me come to the gym with you. Yeah?"

Reed nodded mutely, mouth dry.

Later, Reed would decide that the only flaw in the whole perfect evening was that he couldn't swallow his own inhibitions and kiss Jordan first. He wanted to, but Jordan got there first. He leaned in and did just what Reed had been fantasizing about. This time Jordan wasn't gentle or soft about it; his arm shot up and pinned Reed's shoulder right to the wall, and his lips were so insistent and certain, Reed was immediately swept away by Jordan's desire, his own growing to match in only a handful of moments.

They kissed for a long time against the wall, Reed's knees turning to jelly as Jordan sank deeper and closer into him, their bodies molding together until it felt like all that was holding Reed upright was the strong thigh Jordan had wedged between them.

Reed didn't want the moment to end, because for the first time in so many years, the chatter in his brain faded and he simply felt instead. He didn't second-guess himself as his hands slid up Jordan's back, pulling his shirt from his pants and letting his palms soak up the burning heat of Jordan's skin.

Jordan ripped away Reed's shirt, fingers circling one pectoral muscle and then unexpectedly pinching a nipple. Reed moaned into Jordan's mouth. It was like they'd already had the uncomfortable conversation about sexual preferences, and they'd also avoided the first date awkwardness entirely by skipping right ahead to the goodnight kiss.

❧ ☙

It had never occurred to Reed to change things up like this, but it was definitely occurring to him now. His hard cock, aching for something other than the hard press of Jordan's thigh, was making a very strong argument for not stopping.

Then Jordan dropped to his knees, as artlessly graceful as he did everything, both on and off the football field, and pressed his lips to the center of Reed's abs, right below his belly button.

"You're so fucking sexy," he growled into Reed's skin.

Reed rarely felt that way—if he ever had—but he felt that way now. Jordan had helped form that opinion, and the way his tongue was currently tracing every line of his abs was boosting that even more. Reed had never really considered how his gym routine might improve his dating life, but he was rapidly seeing the benefits.

His head tipped back against the wall, and he groaned involuntarily as Jordan's hand strayed to his belt.

"Tell me to stop," Jordan said, and his voice sounded wrecked, like he was arguing with himself. And he might as well have been, because Reed definitely wasn't going to tell him to stop. Jordan's face was flushed and his fingers shaking a little as he unbuckled Reed's belt and then undid his button fly and lowered the zipper.

Reed didn't know who moaned, but it might have been both of them as Jordan's hand slid hot and certain over his cock, still trapped in his boxer briefs.

"Tell me to stop," Jordan asked again, this time the demand in his voice wavering. Like he was losing the fight. Reed had already lost it, if he'd ever had it to begin with. He didn't know why Jordan was even asking, until he kept talking. "I wanted to take you out, treat you right, make sure you knew I liked you, not just wanted to fuck you," he said, almost like he was talking to himself. Trying to insist to himself. But the whole time, his fingers were stroking Reed's cock through his underwear, driving him crazy.

"You are, you are," was all Reed could insist back, breathless and panting at the pleasure spiking through him.

Reed knew the moment Jordan lost the battle. His eyes turned hot and decisive, and he pulled down Reed's underwear, and his world suddenly narrowed to the white-hot heat of Jordan's mouth and his clever fingers, digging into his thighs.

The pain almost helped to ground him as Jordan's tongue wrapped around the head of his cock, wringing every ounce of pleasure that he could out of Reed.

Reed found he couldn't even be self-conscious at how quickly his orgasm was approaching. His hand reached towards Jordan and his fingers sifted through his hair, giving a quick tug when it became impossible to resist the urge to fall over the edge.

They'd both fallen off the edge, Reed realized in a daze, as he noticed the wet spot on the front of Jordan's jeans.

"You smell so good and you taste even better," Jordan said, his voice even rougher. Reed finally let his knees lose their battle with gravity and he slid to the floor next to Jordan. He leaned over and kissed him, tasting himself on Jordan's tongue.

"I didn't mean to do that," Jordan repeated after Reed pulled away. "I really didn't. But you answered the door, and god damn, you are a work of art. I couldn't wait any longer to get my hands on you."

Reed flushed. "That's not all you had on me," he mumbled.

Jordan laughed, the sound loud in the quiet loft. "I'm going to get you for that," he said, but he sounded more amused than annoyed.

"I sure hope so," Reed admitted shyly, and pulled Jordan close, tucking him in between his knees, and resting his chin on Jordan's shoulder. "Because I like you a lot too."

"You know we could still go out . . ." Jordan said hesitantly, and then paused. But Reed already knew what he wanted—because Reed wanted the exact same thing. He wanted to pick Jordan up and take him to his bed and only leave when the pizza they'd ordered showed up at the front door.

Pizza, beer, a few late-night episodes of bad TV. And Jordan, next to him. Making him laugh, hearing him talk about his life. That was the perfect date to Reed.

This time, he didn't overthink it, he just said it. His heart thudded a little harder at the end of the question, but maybe that was because Jordan had just blown his mind—and his cock.

Reed knew that Jordan couldn't possibly know yet how difficult some social interactions were for him, but he still didn't leave Reed waiting a second longer than he had to. He only said, "That sounds perfect to me, too," and his hand strayed up to where Reed's was clutching his shoulder, covering it with his own, squeezing reassuringly.

❦ ❦

Present day

Way behind on his Secret Santa responsibilities, Reed finally found the time to pop a Christmas card in the mail along with a gift certificate for a hot stone massage. It wasn't as cute as leaving it on Jemma's desk as a surprise after a long meeting, but she was out until mid-January with the wedding and honeymoon. Jordan had mentioned she'd be back for the Christmas party and Secret Santa reveal, but that she was out of the office otherwise.

Reed felt a little guilty that he'd let so much time go between gifts, but with *Dream Team* about to head into filming their next season of episodes, *plus* the whole Jordan thing, Reed was more frazzled than he liked to admit to.

Nick had finally approved the double Italian dinner party episode. As far as Reed was concerned, the disposable container of tiramisu that he had left on Nick's desk must have been the tipping point. He usually preferred cooking from his own knowledge or formulating his own recipes, but even Reed couldn't deny that Quentin's tiramisu recipe was delicious.

With *Dream Team* filming approaching, Reed hadn't had any more date opportunities with Jordan, but they made the most of their time together, often grabbing dinner to go and sitting at one of the big conference tables, notes spread over the surface, as they finalized details of the upcoming episodes.

Reed knew the moment Landon and Quentin figured out what Jordan's ultimate plan was on the dinner party episode. It was blatant from their stony expressions as they walked into one of the last meetings before filming began.

"We know what you're trying to do," Landon said. He crossed his arms over his chest, trying–and mostly failing–to look tough.

Jordan raised an eyebrow. "What am I trying to do?"

Quen broke in. "That whole laid-back bullshit isn't going to work." Reed couldn't remember ever hearing Quen talk this way. "You know, that whole thing where you convince us to repeat what you're doing and it sounds like we're the ones overreacting."

"You totally do that," Reed said, and then nearly clapped a hand over his mouth. He hadn't meant to say that out loud, but it was something Jordan did that had always annoyed the crap out of Reed.

It was surprisingly satisfying to hear that he wasn't alone in his dislike.

Jordan shot Reed a look that was nearly a glare, and he couldn't help but squirm in his chair. Like Quentin, Jordan didn't really have much of a temper, but when he got mad, it was a sudden, hot explosion.

"You asked me to be on your show," Jordan said silkily. "I agreed, even though it was a painfully transparent attempt to get me into the same vicinity as my ex-boyfriend. I thought I was doing you a favor and you wouldn't mind doing me a solid back."

"You should be grateful we agreed to help you at all," Landon exclaimed.

Reed had an inkling they were actually arguing about him and he didn't like it at all.

"You mean, *I* agreed to *let* you help me," Jordan corrected.

Yeah, they were definitely arguing about him.

"That doesn't matter now," Reed broke in. "We're both . . . grateful, I guess. But it's done. Or nearly done. We're figuring our relationship out. The main issue is that Jordan wants to use your show as a platform. Are you going to let him?"

He watched as Landon and Quentin exchanged silent looks.

Reed remembered how Landon had come out all those years ago and that the reaction hadn't been great. From the moment Jordan had told him what he intended to do, he'd fully expected some push back from Landon and Quen, but he'd also expected that Landon would come around to a fully supportive position.

And wherever Landon went, Quentin was almost sure to follow.

"We were just surprised," Landon said, the wind going right out of his sails.

"Yeah, we had to fight for the show to even be ours," Quentin added.

That wasn't how Jordan had described it happening, but Reed could tell from his expression that he was going to let that comment go. After all, he was basically pre-empting part of Landon and Quentin's show. Yes, they'd given him the opening by asking him to appear, but Reed also believed that Jordan wouldn't have done it if the three of them weren't all on the same page.

"So we're good?" Reed asked.

"We're good," Landon agreed, a smile even breaking through his stony expression. "And for the record, we're both very happy for you, Jordan."

Jordan shot them a quick smile, and then went onto the other finalizing items on the agenda. He might look cool and collected, but Reed knew him better–better than anyone did. He knew Jordan had been uncharacteristically nervous about it. Not only how Landon and Quen might take it, but coming out in general. Reed remembered very clearly how apprehensive Jordan had sounded at even the possibility, and that had only been two years ago. Yes, he was less in the public sphere now than he'd been then, but he was still planning to do this in a very public way.

After the meeting, Landon and Quen ran off, Landon because he had some studio time he wanted to fit in, and Quentin because he never *didn't* want to check in on the bakery. It left Jordan and Reed alone.

Reed took a deep breath. "I want you to know you don't have to do this for me. Last time, it was . . . fine that you weren't out. If you're not ready, there's no reason to rush it. I'm happy to take things at your pace."

Jordan looked up in surprise. "I'm not doing it for you," he said.

"You hide it really well, because that's who you are," Reed said, "but I can tell how apprehensive this makes you." He wasn't Jordan's boyfriend–not yet, anyway–but he was always going to be a friend.

Reed could see he wanted to argue, wanted to deny it, but instead, he gave in, and sunk back into the chair he'd been occupying during the meeting. When he met Reed's eyes, he'd let all the fear bubble to the surface.

"Someone once told me that anything worth doing is also worth a little fear."

"That was me," Reed said steadily. "When you tried to convince me that signing up for *Kitchen Wars* was a terrible idea."

"Would you do it again?"

"*Kitchen Wars?*"

Jordan gave a short laugh. "No. Come out."

Reed hesitated, then sat down too. They'd never explicitly discussed this before; they'd never had the chance. Everything had been fairy-tale perfect the way a brand-new relationship is for the first few months, and then instead of dealing with the normal shit they might have encountered, Jordan had been traded to the Los Angeles Rams.

"I came out in high school, and I was really stupid." Reed didn't like talking about it, but he knew Jordan deserved to hear this part of his past. A part he'd chosen not to share when they'd dated before.

"You probably weren't that stupid," Jordan said. "If I know you at all, I'd guess that you just wanted to be honest. You didn't think through what others might say, all you cared about was being truthful.”

“It’s weird how well you know me,” Reed grumbled.

“So I’m right?”

“Of course you’re right. There was a girl who liked me. I was fifteen? Sixteen? And I didn’t want her to get the wrong idea, because I already knew I wasn’t going to like her that way. So I told her. I guess it never occurred to me she might tell everyone or that anyone might care.”

“High school kids are the worst,” Jordan said sympathetically. Reed was discovering that telling Jordan wasn’t like telling other people. But then he’d always been the exception of every one of Reed’s rules. “Bullies and cliques and ignorance.”

“It wasn’t actually the kids who were the worst,” Reed admitted wryly. “My best friend’s parents, they freaked out and thought I might try to ‘corrupt’ their son.”

It had been almost fifteen years since Reed had been told he couldn’t see his best friend anymore. He’d assumed while the scar tissue might still sting occasionally, it had closed and healed. Jordan’s look of empathy both wrenched the stitches and also managed to soothe the wound in ways Reed had never discovered.

There had been so many reasons why Reed had been angry at the world after losing *Kitchen Wars*. It wasn’t even the loss that hurt anymore, but what the loss had represented. No West Coast-based Garnet. A long-distance relationship with very little end in sight. And ultimately no Jordan.

That had been the real loss. Reed had never let people get particularly close, but he'd let this man into his heart and it had been effortless. He couldn't even remember making a decision about it. It had just *happened*. And then he'd lost him.

"You didn't even like your best friend, did you? It was someone else," Jordan guessed, because he was blessed with magical powers where Reed was concerned. Always had been.

"It was the older brother of the girl," Reed said. "That's why I told her. It didn't seem right otherwise."

"Why didn't you tell me this before?" Jordan asked.

"You didn't want to come out then. I figured we had time to talk about it eventually."

Jordan shot to his feet and started pacing back and forth behind the conference table. Reed could tell he was both uneasy and determined. "I'm doing this because like you said, it doesn't seem right otherwise. I'm sick of lying. I'm terrified to do it, but I'm more terrified of what I'll become if I keep hiding it."

"You've thought it through. You know exactly what you're doing. You think it's the right thing to do. So you should do it."

Jordan stopped behind Reed's chair and rested his hands on the other man's shoulders. He tipped his head down, laying it on Reed's. "Thank you for always saying the right thing."

Before Reed could protest that he knew he definitely didn't always say the right thing, Jordan continued. "I'm glad you're going to be there. I mean, Landon and Quen are good friends. They get it too. But they're not you."

This time Reed didn't have to say a word, they were on the exact same page. He turned and kissed Jordan, reaching up to tug him down, always closer.

Chapter Eight

Jordan came in early the next morning. He'd slept surprisingly well–the credit for that had to go to Reed, who, per usual, knew the perfect thing to say when he was struggling. Jordan knew Reed believed he was too honest, too blunt, and definitely too awkward in his delivery. But what made other people uncomfortable had always made Jordan feel safe. He never had to worry about ulterior motives with Reed. He never waited for the other shoe to drop.

He stopped by Starbucks, picking up a coffee for himself and a huge iced tea for Reed. It was going to be a long day. Landon and Quentin might have become easier to film with after Jordan had started working with them, but they still weren't *easy*. Add in himself and Reed to the mix, and even with all the planning they had done for this long episode, Jordan knew there were going to be extremely trying moments.

Reed might have filmed *Kitchen Wars* with Landon and Quentin, but *Dream Team* was a whole different beast. No matter how much Jordan might warn him about today, the only way for Reed to truly see was to experience it.

He left the iced tea in the center of Reed's desk. He noticed when he set it down that the "J" the baristas usually wrote on his coffee was clearly written on the side of Reed's cup.

Oh well. It wasn't like Reed probably didn't already suspect. He had one more gift stashed away in his office, and originally he hadn't planned on giving it to Reed yet, but maybe he should. There were only a few more days until the Christmas party and he might not get many more opportunities during filming.

Jordan slunk back to his office, grabbed one of two remaining gift bags and set it next to the iced tea. The "J" scrawled across the curve of the cup was obvious, but if Reed couldn't figure out that Jordan was his Secret Santa after opening the gift bag, he didn't know what else to do.

He'd bought the scarf three months ago, when he was supposed to have gotten over Reed already, and before Nick had ever considered that *Five Points* needed a culinary director.

One cloudy day in September, Landon had insisted he "call in sick" and come with him and Quen to the newly opened Harry Potter park at Universal Studios. He'd told himself even as he bought the scarf with its distinctive colors that it was stupid and useless. He wasn't ever going to see Reed again, and even if he did, they'd never again be in a place where this gift might be appropriate.

But he'd kept it in his closet anyway, the physical manifestation of all the hope that he couldn't seem to extinguish completely.

Two years earlier

Jordan thought Reed looked delicious in his glasses. He only wore them late at night, in bed reading, and in the early mornings. When Jordan had asked once why he didn't wear them more often—after all, he looked insanely hot in them—Reed had just laughed and said, "How am I supposed to cook at Garnet in glasses?"

Jordan had conceded the point, but he still liked looking at Reed in them.

Right now, they were lying in bed, Reed reading a book, Jordan scrolling aimlessly through Twitter on his tablet.

"You read a lot, don't you?" Jordan asked. They'd only been together a few months, and they were still in that exciting period where he kept learning brand-new things about his lover. One, Reed still liked reading actual books. Two, Reed seemed to have a different book every time they were in bed together, which was becoming increasing in its frequency–a state of affairs that Jordan had absolutely zero problem with.

Reed glanced up from the page he was absorbed in. "I've always liked it."

Leveraging himself more upright, Jordan read the title on the cover. It was a Tom Clancy thriller. He'd seen Reed in bed with cookbooks, *Game of Thrones*, bestsellers, two Rick Riordan books, and a bunch of others that he'd never heard of before.

"What's your favorite book?" Jordan asked, thinking that for anyone who read as much and as widely as Reed, that might be a difficult question.

But Reed answered immediately and with absolute certainty. "Harry Potter."

"I've never read them, only seen the movies," Jordan said, reaching over and sliding a thumb down the spine of the paperback. "I bet you're going to tell me that they're a lot better."

"Oh, much, much better," Reed said, a grin on his face. "Did you ever take that quiz on Pottermore that told you which Hogwarts house you'd be sorted into?"

"Potter-what?" Jordan asked. In the last three months, he'd discovered that not only was Reed a voracious learner for all things culinary, he absorbed so much of the world. Other people might have called him a nerd, but frankly, Jordan was usually in awe of how much he knew.

"It's a website that sort of gives you a deep dive into the world of Harry Potter," Reed said. "And there's a quiz where it'll tell you what house you'd be in at Hogwarts."

This was one of the things that Jordan loved most about Reed—he opened his horizons, consistently and effortlessly, because he wasn't ever really trying. He just *was*, this incredibly fascinating and complex individual. Serious and earnest and insanely smart, but then he'd turn around and tell a dirty joke worthy of one of Jordan's frat brothers.

It didn't take long for Jordan to switch out of Twitter on his tablet, and navigate to the Pottermore site. He answered the questions, and then the result popped up on the screen.

"What!" he exclaimed, even though he hadn't meant to say anything at all. It was just such a . . . surprise.

"What is it?" Reed asked, leaning over and looking at the screen of Jordan's tablet. "Oh, you're a Slytherin. I could've guessed that."

"A Slytherin!" Jordan cried. "Aren't they the bad ones?"

"I can't believe you," Reed said in mock horror. "Get rid of your filthy Slytherin prejudice, we don't want any of it here."

"Well, which house is yours, then?" Jordan grumbled.

"Oh, that's easy. Ravenclaw." Reed sounded enormously pleased with this answer. "Though I can see how I could've been sorted in Hufflepuff."

"You've put some thought into this." Jordan didn't know why he was so surprised.

"Of course," Reed said, like everyone seriously considered what house they might be sorted into at Hogwarts.

A year later, Jordan was standing in one of the stores at Harry Potter World, and couldn't help but gravitate right towards the Ravenclaw scarves with their distinctive blue striping. He'd already grabbed a green one for himself, because after some research he'd learned that Slytherin wasn't all bad and that the Pottermore site had definitely been right about where he belonged.

There was a very good chance he'd never see Reed again. He'd never forget him even if he didn't. He'd never forget that conversation in bed. And he'd definitely never forgive himself for letting a man like that go.

He bought the scarf and refused to discuss it with Landon, who had been both perplexed and insanely curious as to why he needed two. Even though it was almost seventy degrees, Landon had proudly wound his Gryffindor scarf around his neck and had harassed Quentin until he'd done the same with his yellow and black striped one.

"Now," Landon had said, "if we can only find our mysterious Ravenclaw, we'll have a full Hogwarts complement."

Jordan had never told Landon that the Ravenclaw was Reed, but he had a feeling that Landon had eventually guessed.

Present day

It was weird instead of hanging behind the camera in jeans and a t-shirt with his hair hidden by a Chicago Bears hat, Jordan was forced to undergo makeup and hair with Landon and Quen. Then there was the ordeal of having his clothes fussed over. He'd brought a selection of shirts, assuming that he could pair whatever was picked with his best pair of dark wash jeans.

"But it's a party!" Landon had cried when he'd spotted Jordan's choices. The problem was that next to the polka-dotted rainbow bowtie Landon was wearing, everything looked boring.

"You're just going to be festive for the rest of us," Reed had inserted, and Jordan would have to be deaf not to tell that he was running interference.

As Jordan pulled off his shirt and shrugged on a leaf-green short-sleeved button-up, the look Reed shot him was warm, bordering on hot. It looked a lot like the former, but Jordan had a feeling if he had asked him, he'd say it was both.

"We actually got you both something," Landon said. "It's a party, after all."

At least Quentin had the intelligence to look embarrassed as he distributed the gift bags. Jordan watched as Reed pulled out a bright rainbow pin that on anyone else might dwarf their chest, but on Reed took up about a quarter of his pec.

"Oh, thanks," Reed said, barely holding to the charade, "I've always wanted a . . . flashing rainbow pin."

"And now you, Jordan," Landon said, and he sounded far too excited. Also, far too pleased with himself. Jordan was only now beginning to realize that even after Landon had quit matchmaking, he wasn't the type to ever just chill.

Jordan pulled a bright rainbow feather boa out of his bag. "Oh geez, guys, you didn't have to," he said. "And I mean, *you really didn't have to.*"

Landon shrugged. "I thought it might help move things along. And–Quen! You're not wearing yours!" Quentin's expression turned sheepish and he drew on a rainbow beanie over his blond curls. "Now, we're all set. I thought it might be nice. Supportive and all that."

"I'll take it as a win that we're not all dressed as Carmen Miranda," Reed said. Clearly, he had been watching old episodes of *Dream Team* because Quen had dressed up with a fruit headpiece in one of the early ones.

"That headdress was fantastic," Landon sniffed. "And Quen looked so good in it."

"I think you liked it because it had built-in snacking potential," Quen drawled back.

"Thank you, really. I appreciate it a lot," Jordan said. He'd written himself several openings into the script. It hadn't been hard considering that Landon and Quentin's conversations usually ran to the gayer side of the spectrum. Jordan had planned on waiting for the right moment to use them, but as he draped the boa around his neck, maybe that was all unnecessary.

Landon looked ridiculous with his bowtie but the look on his face was as sincere and supportive as he'd ever seen it. Jordan didn't know whether he wanted to cry or puke with nerves.

Luckily, that was the moment the set assistant showed up to usher them to Landon and Quentin's fake kitchen.

Season two meant a bigger set, which was good, because the old one had been cramped with only Landon and Quentin. Adding in Reed and Jordan would have probably been a disaster. Now, they all just barely fit.

"You okay?" Reed turned and asked into Jordan's ear as they got the lighting finalized.

"I'm good," Jordan said. It was almost true.

"Whatever you need me for," Reed said. "I'm here."

"Anything?" Jordan asked, arching an eyebrow suggestively.

Reed just smiled.

"What about a kiss?" Jordan persisted. Yes, he was wearing an enormous rainbow feather boa. Yes, he had been flirting his ass off with Reed over the last few weeks. But he hadn't technically come out at work yet. This was a big episode, highly anticipated, and there were definitely more staff than usual floating around at the back of the set. Gossip made the rounds just as quickly at *Five Points* as it did other workplaces, so anyone who wasn't here would hear about it soon.

Reed didn't say anything. He just looked, seriously and solemnly, at Jordan, then leaned in.

It wasn't a quick peck, and it wasn't a long, drawn-out affair—not like what Jordan secretly craved having again whenever he wanted it—but even though it fell near the middle of the kiss spectrum, Jordan felt it to his toes. And when Reed released him and the roaring in his ears had stopped, he could hear the quiet that had fallen around the set.

"You two," Landon's voice pierced through the silence. "Can't leave you alone for one blessed minute."

It was exactly what Jordan had found himself saying to Landon and Quentin many, *many* times during the filming of season one, and he couldn't help it. He burst into laughter.

Jordan wasn't naïve enough to believe that coming out was a simple or a straightforward process–he'd seen too many friends experience it to believe otherwise, but it still felt easy. A kiss and a joke and some shared laughter, and when Jordan glanced around the set, there wasn't a shred of judgement on anyone's face. He'd not really expected to see much, considering who ran the whole site, but still, the love and acceptance on so many faces was the last bit of reassurance he needed to move forward.

❧ ☙

"Welcome to *Dream Team*," Landon said, "I'm Landon Patton, and this is my favorite partner in crime, Quentin Maxwell."

So far so good, Reed thought. He never felt particularly comfortable in front of the camera, which was why he knew so many of his friends had been surprised when he'd decided to do *Kitchen Wars*. He'd turned down so many television offers before that, local, regional and even national shows. He'd never been interested in being the center of attention, only the center of people's palates.

"Today, we have a special surprise for you," Quen said, picking up smoothly where Landon left off. If you listened to them, you'd probably correctly guess that they'd rehearsed about a hundred times. They actually had and Reed had been present for most of the rehearsals. "Our good friends, Jordan Christensen and Reed Ryan."

"We're going to teach Jordan some fun kitchen tricks for a great dinner party. As for Reed, we're going to hope that he doesn't embarrass us too much," Landon added with a big smile for the camera.

"Hey, babe, speak for yourself," Quen teased back, nudging his boyfriend with a playful shoulder bump. "I bet I could hold my own with Reed."

"You wish," Reed joined in, because something about having Jordan at his side relaxed him, and made him more able to add to the cute banter that Landon and Quen had going. Under the cover of the kitchen counter, Jordan's hand reached out and gently bumped his thigh. Reed knew it was a "good job" pat for improvising and participating.

"Are we done measuring dicks yet?" Jordan teased. "'Cause I'm starving."

Everyone laughed, even some of the crew, which didn't surprise Reed at all. One of the things he'd always loved about Jordan was his sharp sense of humor, as well as his ability to dish back a perfect comment almost instantaneously. Reed was one of the few who knew that particular retort hadn't been scripted.

Reed was happy because they hadn't had to stop the camera yet. With the extra rehearsals under their belt, the idea had been to get through the opening quickly, with only one or two takes. Normally the plan was to film two to three episodes in a day—and it was a very long day, too—but everyone had agreed that with the extra additions to the set and the extended length, they'd be lucky to get through this particular episode in a single day.

"I get asked a lot what chefs do when they have less time to prepare meals. Since our schedules got busier—Landon touring and in the studio, and me at the bakery—taking a few hours to cook dinner isn't always an option. So, what do chefs do to save time and energy in the kitchen? Reed?"

Reed leaned on the counter and tried to seem casual like this was a conversation he might normally have with Quentin and not because Jordan had written the words coming out of his mouth. "I try to base my meals around quality ingredients. If you have good building blocks to start with, dinner doesn't have to be complicated or take forever to make."

The director called cut, and they set up for the next shot. It wasn't his job to make sure each ingredient was where it needed to be, but it had always been tough for Reed to delegate, and he spent the next few minutes checking over the *mise en place* that his employees had set up, making sure everything was perfect for the next segment.

Quentin was getting better at talking about food, and easier in front of the camera, Reed thought as he talked about marinating store-bought mozzarella to serve as an appetizer. Whenever he'd gotten decent internet, he'd always made sure to check *Five Points* to see if a new episode of *Dream Team* was up. He'd never blamed Quentin or Landon for booting him out of *Kitchen Wars*. He'd never even blamed Rory, and Rory had won the whole damn thing. Reed had only blamed himself–still did, a little, if he was being really honest with himself. He was a great chef; it didn't matter that ultimately the show hadn't been about culinary skills, his abilities should have made sure he came out on top.

During the first few episodes, Quen had been hesitant, still deferring to Landon, even during some of the more advanced cooking segments, but now, he was confidently addressing the camera, describing what a typical day and evening might be like for him and Landon.

Jordan had mentioned during one of their meetings how, for so many who watched the show, the draw wasn't really the food Quentin and Landon cooked. It was the glimpse into the lives of two charismatic and deeply in love people. When Reed had asked if the stories Jordan was writing were true, he'd shrugged and said they were "true enough."

Reed couldn't blame his friends for wanting to keep some of their private life private. It was something he'd struggled with when dating Jordan before, and back then the world had only known him as a good friend. Now, it was inevitable that the truth was going to come out, along with Jordan. Reed would need to get used to the idea of being half of a well-known couple.

He wasn't looking forward to it, even as he desperately wanted to resume his relationship with Jordan.

"Some evenings," Quentin said as he drizzled in olive oil over the mozzarella, "we'll just snack if we're too tired to cook. I never thought I'd be too tired to whip something up, but the truth is, life is hard and busy. And spending time with Landon is more important than always making sure we have a gourmet meal."

"Sometimes we even cook together," Landon added. He turned to Jordan and Reed, a glint in his eye that never promised good things. "What about you and Jordan, Reed?"

Here it was. The moment of truth. Reed could feel Jordan tense next to him. He'd not wanted to reveal Jordan's sexuality by outing their relationship–past or present–but here was the opportunity and Landon was serving it up on a silver platter.

He fully expected the director to call cut. But instead of letting the silence drag on too long and force him to, Jordan spoke up. "Nice job, Landon. You totally let the cat out of the bag." He smiled directly at the camera, and Reed didn't think he'd ever seen the other man so confident or sure of himself. It radiated out of every pore on his skin, and he glowed with it. Reed had never realized how much hiding cost Jordan, but seeing him reveal himself was almost like seeing a brand-new Jordan.

"Yes," Jordan admitted. "I'm not just wearing this boa to be supportive. I definitely like cute boys. You happy now?" He slid an inquisitive glance in Landon's direction.

"If you kiss that cute boy over there, I'd be a lot happier," Landon said.

"This cute boy?" Jordan asked innocently, leaning over to poke Quentin in the shoulder. Quentin, who was chopping herbs, didn't even react. Reed's own stomach was jumping with nerves. He knew exactly who Landon wanted Jordan to kiss.

Him.

"Not that one," Landon said with a laugh. "That one's mine. Get your own cute boy."

"How about this one?" Jordan said, and his husky voice was suddenly very close to Reed's ear. He'd been tasked to separate the eggs for the tiramisu, and his hand trembled on the egg. He set it down and couldn't help but glance up into Jordan's eyes. He looked very sure, and Reed wasn't certain he could have gone along with it otherwise.

"Good choice!" Landon called out, and Reed heard it in the distance as Jordan closed the space between them, leaning down to kiss him.

Reed had sort of expected Jordan to keep it mild. At least milder than the kiss they'd shared pre-filming.

He didn't.

Jordan wrapped his arms around Reed's shoulders and pulled them flush, kissing him with a burning determination. Reed couldn't help but remember that first time they'd kissed, him pushed up against the kitchen counter, Jordan's hands wandering everywhere, his desire clear.

His desire was just as obvious right now.

"This is the gayest site on the internet," Landon announced happily.

Reed wondered in a distant corner of his mind–the only bit not consumed by Jordan–if Landon had won the bet and that's why he sounded so pleased with himself.

They broke apart and Jordan's smile was radiant. Reed thought it couldn't be as big as his own that was currently threatening to break his face in two.

The director yelled cut.

Probably because they'd gone too long without actually doing or saying anything about cooking. They were so far off script it wasn't even funny, and for the first time today, Reed discovered he didn't give a damn.

❧ ❧

"That was a long-ass day," Jordan grumbled as they walked into Reed's office. "A good day, but a fucking ridiculous one."

"When the day starts with you wearing a rainbow feather boa, it can only get more ridiculous from there," Reed pointed out.

He glanced over at his desk, looking for his phone and his keys, and he spotted the bag that he'd caught a glimpse of this morning but hadn't had time to open.

A Secret Santa gift. A Secret Santa gift that he was nearly sure by now was from Jordan. The enormous "J" written on the side of his iced tea this morning had only solidified Reed's suspicions.

"Oh, look, a Secret Santa present," Jordan said, his voice completely transparent. "You should open it."

"You realize you're not fooling anyone," Reed said good-naturedly. Even after how long today had been, he couldn't be annoyed. Not when he was so happy he burned with it.

"I don't know what you're talking about. The Secret Santa reveal isn't for another two days. Everything is locked down until then."

"Yeah, yeah, whatever," Reed grumbled. He opened the bag because he couldn't imagine Jordan was going to let them leave this office until he did, even though they'd both been here for at least twelve hours.

He reached in, and pulled out the contents. The breath went out of his lungs.

It was one thing to know that Jordan was buying him these gifts, and it was another to *know*.

"This is a Ravenclaw scarf," he said stupidly because his brain had time-traveled to a time before when they'd been so perfectly, completely happy. He was happy now, but that had been a different kind of happiness. A happiness without fear or anger or pain. It was the happiness of a fairy tale that couldn't last, and like clockwork, reality had burst the bubble. But here was the ideal memento from that halcyon time.

"Yes, it is," Jordan said steadily. "I have a Slytherin one to match."

Reed was nearly in tears. "Was I really supposed to get this and not know it was from you?"

Jordan must have known because he dropped everything he was carrying and was around Reed's desk in a heartbeat, pulling him into his arms. "You were definitely supposed to know," Jordan said quietly into Reed's ear. "I wanted to give you . . . something special. I wanted you to know how special you are to me, after I spent way too long not telling you. I know it can't make up for the past, but I wanted to try."

"You remembered," Reed said, and yeah, that was definitely a wet spot on Jordan's shoulder.

"I couldn't forget," Jordan said softly. "I bought this long before you were offered this job. When I saw it, I couldn't leave it on the shelf."

Reed didn't think his voice would be very steady, but it came out surprisingly certain. "Jordan, take me home."

"Right now?" he squeaked out. The laid-back, cooler-than-you persona he'd cultivated had long shattered. Reed *always* saw the real Jordan.

"We've been waiting almost two years. Don't you think that's long enough?"

Jordan didn't even need a moment to consider. "Yes."

He reached out and grabbed Reed's hand, practically dragged him down the hallway to the elevator, and then down to the parking lot, not letting go of him even for a second.

"What about my car?" Reed asked as Jordan, caught up in a single-minded need to get them somewhere private, pulled them towards his Lexus. "I have to work tomorrow."

Jordan paused, his hand on the door handle. "Call in sick?" he asked hopefully, one of those lopsided smiles lighting his features.

Shaking his head, Reed wanted to laugh, but Jordan was hard enough to dissuade on the worst days; on the best, he was impossible. "You're incorrigible," he teased.

"How about this," Jordan said, leaning over the roof of the car, his expression morphing from playful to intense, "if you still feel like getting out of bed when I'm done with you, I'll drive you to work."

Reed swallowed hard. "Deal."

Jordan nodded succinctly and got into the car. Reed followed, his blood singing with anticipation.

It was a seven-minute drive from the *Five Points* office to Reed's apartment. Jordan made it in four.

When they reached Reed's apartment and some much-needed privacy, Reed asked, "Do you remember the first time we did this?" as he unlocked the door.

Jordan shot him a disbelieving look. "Um. *Yes.*"

"I've been thinking about it," Reed said, and then blushed. Because yeah, he'd been thinking about him and Jordan having sex. Sometimes it was difficult *not* to think about it, but that wasn't entirely what he'd meant. "I mean, not the sex, but yeah, that too, if I'm honest."

Jordan settled his hands on Reed's shoulders. "I think about it too, it's sort of hard to forget something so memorable," he said, meeting his gaze with no hesitation or embarrassment. "Which part of it? The way we were supposed to go out to dinner and I came to pick you up but instead of actually leaving your place, we ended up making out next to your front door?"

Reed couldn't help it, he blushed again.

"Or," Jordan said, his eyes hot and calculating, like he knew exactly what he was doing to Reed, "how we had sex on the floor because we couldn't even make it to the bed?" His hand slid up Reed's thigh, just skirting where Reed's cock was hard and pressing against his zipper.

"I wouldn't change it," Reed admitted. "It was perfect even if my knees felt it for a week. But this is a fresh start. A new beginning . . ."

"Bed this time?" Jordan asked hopefully, his hand moving around the curve of Reed's waist, pulling him close.

Reed's only answer was to kiss him, his hands cradling Jordan's head at just the right angle.

It took three-ish attempts to make it to the bedroom, which was only a few yards away from the front door. By the time they actually made it to the bed, they'd both lost their shirts, Reed was sucking a bruise into the crook of Jordan's neck and Jordan's hands had wandered under Reed's jeans, and under his briefs, sliding over the curve of his ass.

"Missed this, missed *you*," Jordan panted as they wiggled out of pants, still reluctant to let go of each other. "Wanna see you."

Reed shucked the rest of his jeans with his underwear and crawled up the bed, flopping over and meeting Jordan's eyes as he looked his fill.

"Nobody would ever guess that you were the chef and I was the professional athlete," Jordan said, his words casual but his tone gravelly rough as his fingertips traced the defined curves of Reed's abs, the swell of his pectorals.

"I've been stressed," Reed admitted, shuddering as Jordan's fingers grazed a nipple.

"Despite the beauty that your stress creates," Jordan said, "I'm going to try to eliminate most of that."

"Not all of it?" Reed joked as Jordan crawled up his body. He was doing his own teasing, brushing his hard cock against Jordan's in tantalizing but unsatisfactory ways. Reed wanted so much more.

"I'm only a man, baby," he teased right back, his lips meeting Reed's in a deep, passionate kiss. When it ended, they were panting and eye-to-eye.

"Make love to me," Reed whispered.

"Whatever you want." Jordan's voice was completely sincere, and Reed realized until this moment that he hadn't really believed that Jordan meant it—but he did now. They'd both made their share of mistakes, both screwed up, but now that they'd come together again, they were not only stronger for it, they knew exactly what they wanted.

Each other.

Jordan's hands swept over his body like he was memorizing it, like he'd gotten afraid he might forget it, and was remembering all over again. He opened him up slowly and completely, like Reed was something infinitely precious and he wasn't about to let him break.

And when Reed was just about wild with need, Jordan gave him exactly what he wanted, sliding inside him like he'd never left.

Jordan braced Reed's knee against his shoulder and pushed in deep, Reed's back arching with pleasure. "God, just like that," he panted, as Jordan thrust again and again, his hand slipping down to curl around his sensitive cock.

He remembered just how he liked to be touched, the emotions and the bliss sliding through him in one big wave as Reed fell over the edge, Jordan crying out against his shoulder as he joined him.

Wiped out from a long day and then such an emotionally charged orgasm, Reed lay in bed as Jordan rustled around in the kitchen, probably trying to find something to eat.

He didn't want to get out of bed, but that was *his* kitchen. And Jordan, while fantastic in so many ways, did not possess awesome culinary skills. If he wanted something more than cheese and crackers, he'd need to dig down and find the energy to move.

It took a minute, but his growling stomach won out. He pulled on his briefs and walked into the living room that butted against the open kitchen.

"You don't have to take care of me, you know," Reed said, leaning against the counter.

Jordan, deep in the fridge, popped his head out. "I know," he said, "but you looked pretty much done, and you should eat something before you go to sleep."

"No," Reed said, pulling himself back upright and approaching the fridge, his hand reaching out for Jordan's shoulder. "I know what you're doing. I get it. And you don't have to. There's nothing to make up for. Not anymore."

The expression on Jordan's face made it very clear that Reed had just caught him.

"What if I want to?" Jordan was still Jordan though; incomparably stubborn.

"I forgive you, even if there's not anything to forgive," Reed said.

Jordan crossed his arms over his chest. "I didn't call. I didn't text. I let you *sell* Garnet and disappear into god knows where for however long. I should've told you . . ." His voice got tight and he glanced away. Reed was pretty sure he saw tears glimmering in the corners of his eyes.

"No," Reed repeated, more firmly this time, pulling him against him. "We're both sorry. We both messed up. I shouldn't have left without telling you. You shouldn't have let me go without talking. What we need to do is just let go of the past and move forward."

"That's what I'm trying to do," Jordan said, his head muffled in Reed's chest.

"No, you're trying to make up for what you think is your mistake," Reed said kindly. "The gifts were nice. I loved them. But there's nothing else you need to do."

Jordan pulled back, his eyes watery. "You really mean that."

Reed knew he had a lot of conviction; you didn't make it to the echelon of culinary perfection the way he had without it. He let it all show when he gazed down at the man he loved. "I do mean it. I want you to believe it."

Jordan sighed, the sound of a happy and content man. Reed never wanted to stop hearing it. "I'm working on it, I promise."

Chapter Nine

TWO YEARS EARLIER

It was a night like so many others the last few months.

Reed was in the kitchen at Garnet, whipping up plate after plate of deliciousness that had the city of Chicago as enthralled with him and his talent as they'd ever been.

They weren't alone. Jordan knew he too was as enthralled as he'd ever been—in fact, it felt like he fell deeper, harder, every day.

But he hadn't gone inside, even though he'd promised Reed he'd stop by and let him feed him after practice and a late meeting with his agent. Instead, he was skulking around outside by the tall topiaries, twisted with strands of vivid white lights. The name glowed above the doorway, the muted red still bright against the gloomy sky, cool for May.

He didn't want to go inside because if he did, he would have to tell Reed, and the longer Jordan put it off, the longer he could pretend that reality hadn't dropped a big bucket of cold water onto his damn good life.

It was still going to be pretty good, the problem was that it wasn't going to be in Chicago anymore.

Jordan took a steadying breath and pushed open the door.

Danielle, who ran the front of the house at Garnet, glanced up and instantly smiled as he walked in. "Jordan, it's good to see you," she said, like she didn't end up seeing him most nights. Jordan had been able to persuade Reed to take some time off, but Jordan knew when they'd started dating that Reed *was* Garnet. He wouldn't—he couldn't—dream of taking Reed away from what he'd lovingly created.

Jordan's heart ached.

"He's in the back of the dining room," Danielle said before he could ask. "He's expecting you."

Some nights when it wasn't as busy, Reed would take a break and they'd eat together in a secluded corner of the dining room.

Jordan found him tucked away in the corner they typically used, Reed claiming he didn't want to be interrupted by diners when they ate, Jordan knowing Reed was giving them the privacy Jordan's job required of him. He'd taken off his chef's jacket, his thin white t-shirt straining against the muscles along his spine. Jordan's stomach spun unpleasantly.

"Hey," he said, slipping into the chair opposite his boyfriend.

Reed looked up, a smile transforming his rather ordinary features into something extraordinary. At least, he was always extraordinary to Jordan.

"You're later than you thought you'd be," Reed said, "I hope it was okay that I ordered dinner."

Jordan couldn't tell him that he'd been haunting the front door for half an hour, unable to get the nerve up to actually walk inside. Or that he wasn't actually going to be able to eat.

"My meeting was . . . complicated," Jordan said. Complicated was an understatement.

"You want a glass of wine?"

Jordan braced his hands on his knees underneath the table. Reed hadn't sensed yet that anything was really wrong, but Jordan knew he had a pretty good poker face. "Not that kind of complicated," he said.

Reed's eyes snapped up to his, and now they were worried. "Is everything okay?"

"Remember the meeting I had with my agent a week ago?" Jordan asked and Reed nodded slowly.

"I didn't want to tell you," Jordan continued, "because I didn't want to worry you, but he said he was getting vibes that he wasn't sure the Bears were committed to me next season."

"Something happened today," Reed stated, and even though Jordan hadn't wanted to worry him before, he was definitely worried now.

"I've been traded." His mouth felt like sawdust as the words tumbled out. "To the Los Angeles Rams."

<hr>

"It's gonna be okay, right?" Reed asked for the tenth time so far, his hands moving in a blur, scrubbing a pot Jordan was pretty sure that he'd already scrubbed before.

"It's going to be fine," Jordan said, though he wasn't sure he believed it—and he wasn't sure Reed believed him either. They'd only been together a few months. They were still figuring shit out. They hadn't moved in together yet, even though Jordan wanted to ask him.

They were still suspended in the sparkling perfection of the honeymoon period and now they were both going to have to face the painful edge of reality.

Reed needed to be at his restaurant at least five nights a week. In Chicago.

Jordan was going to be shortly leaving for Los Angeles, where he'd spend the next six months playing for a new team.

Jordan knew he could fly in and visit, but it wasn't going to be the same. He was basically going to be gone for longer than they'd been together.

No wonder Reed was freaking out.

If they'd had a year or two under their belts, if they both felt very certain of themselves and the part they wanted to play in each other's future, Jordan thought they could have done it, no sweat. Now? He wasn't sure, even though he desperately wanted to be.

"We'll figure something out," Reed said, for at least the fifth time in the last hour. He'd moved onto scrubbing the counters again, even though they were already gleaming. *At least he has something to keep his hands busy,* Jordan thought rebelliously, *all I can do is stand here and try to pretend like I'm not freaking out.*

"We totally will," Jordan said, and this time he didn't know if he was comforting Reed or himself.

Maybe they both needed it.

Jordan was finally facing the moving boxes in his loft, shoveling old Bears gear into a box even though he knew he should really get rid of it, when Reed burst in.

"I've got it," he exclaimed, waving his phone around excitedly. "I've figured out what we do. Remember that show that Rory emailed me about? The cooking one?"

"Yeah, the one you read about and then laughed at?" Jordan said skeptically. "The one you said you'd do only if the skin melted off your bones?"

"Yes, that one," Reed said, completely ignoring Jordan's accurate statement. "If I won, I'd have the money to open another Garnet in California."

Jordan set a sweatshirt down. He suddenly felt really old and really tired, and all he wanted was to turn towards the wall and cry. But he couldn't, because he'd been holding it all in, putting on a happy, brave face for Reed.

"You could," Jordan said. "Or you could leave Mike in charge every other week like we talked about." Yeah, they'd talked about it, but Reed had hated the idea. Jordan hadn't thought he'd hated the idea so much that he'd be willing to humiliate himself on a reality TV show, but apparently Reed was keeping some things hidden too.

"It could be the beginning of my restaurant dynasty!" Reed said. "I asked Rory if they'd still be willing to consider me, and he said they were still casting."

Jordan wasn't surprised that he'd been on the producers' initial radar or that they'd still want him. Reed was hot and young and was practically worshipped like a god in Chicago. He'd add a lot of much-needed culinary credibility.

Glancing over at where Jordan was trying to duplicate his excitement, Reed frowned. "This way we could be together a lot more often. I thought you'd be excited."

"Or I could just loan you the fifty thousand dollars," Jordan said, "and then you're not dependent on a stupid TV show to give you the money."

Reed set down his phone with a quiet click onto Jordan's dresser. "I told you I didn't want to take your money."

"I trust you with it, more than anybody else I know," Jordan said. That much was absolutely true. He'd write the check today, right this minute, if he thought there was a chance in hell of Reed taking it.

"That's not how we are," Reed said stubbornly.

"Oh?" Jordan retorted, his temper finally beginning to fray. "And how are we? I thought we were committed to each other? To our future? I thought we were madly in love, and trying to make shit work?"

"We are," Reed insisted.

"All I want is a sure thing," Jordan begged.

"I *am* a sure thing." Reed looked completely confident, as endlessly certain of his own skill in the kitchen.

The problem was that Jordan knew it wasn't only about the food. He might have only been a football player, but he had a pretty good idea of how Hollywood worked. And it wasn't anything like how Reed imagined it did.

Reed took the open spot on *Kitchen Wars.*

He and his partner Diego Flores, a screenwriter famous for his comic book movie adaptations, won third place. Diego went on to write the screenplay for the critically-acclaimed movie, *Suicide Squad.* Reed packed up his knives and went back to Chicago, a sullen shadow of what he'd been when he'd first flown to LA for filming.

And Jordan, who knew he should have texted him or called him or *something* after he got back to Chicago, just . . . didn't.

Present day

"You look . . ." Reed paused in the middle of chopping onions and mushrooms and zucchini, his flying knife stilling as he tried to place Jordan's expression. "Contemplative. Almost a little sad. Let me guess, you're regretting forcing me to call in sick."

"No, no," Jordan laughed, but the smile didn't reach his eyes. "Not at all. Besides, I won; you really didn't want to get out of bed this morning."

"No, I didn't," Reed agreed, and resumed his chopping. "Is something bothering you?"

"I know you forgive me for not calling or not texting after you left LA, but it's hard to forgive myself," Jordan admitted. "And the whole time I kept telling you that everything would be okay after I was traded, I didn't really believe my own bullshit."

"I knew. I knew you were terrified. I was terrified. Neither of us were sure. How could we have been? We'd only been together a few months and suddenly we had to make all these huge decisions," Reed said steadily as he transported the chopped vegetables from cutting board to pan.

"We didn't do a very good job."

"No. And I shouldn't have run off in a huge snit to Chicago. Then the rest of the world," Reed pointed out. "But I'm not going to do it again and I'm going to assume you're not going to stop talking to me again, even when I'm a huge asshole."

Jordan's eyes softened and he smiled, a genuine one this time. "Of course not. Besides, you were only sort of an asshole," he teased.

"Merry Christmas to you too," Reed said. "See if I ever make you another omelet again."

Jordan walked up behind Reed and wrapped him up in his arms. "I want lots and lots of them. For a very long time," he said softly, his tone suddenly very serious.

"As many as you want," Reed said, equally as serious. "Now stop distracting me or we'll never get fed."

⚘

"What's this Christmas party like?" Reed asked as he sat on the edge of Jordan's bed and watched as he pulled on jeans.

Jordan kicked himself internally. He'd forgotten again that Reed didn't typically like big gatherings, and liked lots of reassurances up front that he'd fit in okay. This time he really didn't need to worry, but Jordan should have told him anyway.

"I'm sorry," Jordan said. "I should've . . ."

But Reed just smiled. "You shouldn't be. I'm a grownup. I can handle myself."

"You do, you do great." *Great job, Jordan*, he thought to himself, *you used to know how to do this*. "This" being reassuring Reed without making him feel uncomfortable. In fact, two years ago, it had come naturally and easily, without Jordan even thinking about it. That was only one of the reasons that he'd been so certain that they were meant for each other.

"So tell me what it's like," Reed said.

"It's pretty low-key, honestly," Jordan said, buttoning up his shirt. "Nick always has the taco stand cater, and there's an open bar, and a few strategically placed mistletoe waiting to trip you up. It's not usually a wild night."

"And the Secret Santa reveal," Reed added helpfully with a deceptively innocent smile.

"Oh, yes. Right. The Secret Santa reveal." Jordan prayed that he didn't sound transparent as hell. It was one thing for Reed to have realized he was his Secret Santa—that was so obvious he would've been concerned if Reed hadn't figured it out—but the other thing . . . well . . . that was a little trickier.

He was fairly certain Reed wasn't going to care, but he also didn't want to ruin things just as they'd gotten to a good place again. Per usual, he'd let Landon talk him into something that he didn't know was entirely necessary.

"We should take a cab over," Jordan said. "I've had to walk from the office to my place before and it sucks."

"Who says I'm coming back with you?"

Jordan glanced up in surprise. He'd just *assumed*. Had assumed that Reed wanted to be with him as much as he wanted to be with Reed. Had he read things wrong? Jordan's stomach plummeted to the floor in a sickening swoon, then he glanced up and saw that Reed was smiling, the expression on his face amused. "Of course I'm coming back with you," Reed said. "I can't believe you actually thought I wouldn't want to."

Jordan didn't know what to say. He could've said that things were still so new, and he was still a tiny bit terrified he was going to fuck up again. But when he looked up at Reed he realized he didn't need to. Reed already knew what he was thinking.

"It's going to take awhile," he said, reaching out and snatching Jordan by the waist, wrapping him up tight, his head resting on Jordan's stomach. "But we're going to be okay."

And Jordan believed him.

Reed was just about to request the Uber to pick them up when Jordan walked up behind him. He was carrying a gift bag. Reed opened his mouth to protest—he'd *just* told Jordan the night before that he didn't need to buy his affection or his forgiveness with presents.

"I know, I know," Jordan said wryly. "I don't need to do this. But I want to." He extended the bag in Reed's direction. "Merry Christmas."

"What's this?" Reed asked, gently pulling the tissue paper out of the bag. "Your last Secret Santa gift?"

Jordan just shrugged. "Open it and see."

The paper drifted to the floor like snowflakes as Reed pulled more from the bag. Finally, he lifted a hardbound book out. That Jordan would give him a book wasn't all that surprising.

What was surprising and left him somewhat speechless was that the picture on the cover was a picture of the two of them, Jordan nestled in the crook of Reed's neck, his smile light and carefree and blindingly happy. Reed couldn't help but remember how he'd felt when they'd taken that picture. They'd only been dating a few weeks, maybe even less, and it was probably one of their first pictures together. The more he thought about it, he was sure it *was* the first. He still had that awestruck look in his eyes, the one that spoke volumes about how he couldn't believe Jordan Christensen wanted to give him the time of day.

"That's the first picture we ever took together," Jordan said quietly. "The very first."

Reed looked up at Jordan, his forehead creased in confusion. "Is this . . . this about us?"

"Just look," Jordan said, so Reed had no choice but to open the book.

As he flipped through the pages, there were more memories preserved there—more than he'd even remembered. Reed's fingertips brushed one of the pictures—one of them and Rory from when he'd come to Chicago, smiles bright like they believed they could conquer the world. Another of just the two of them, from the very beginning, when they'd been goofing around naked in bed and Jordan had insisted on taking a selfie. Reed's eyes were dark and slumbering, satisfied and happy, his arm slung around Jordan's bare shoulders.

"I didn't even know you had this many pictures of us," Reed said wonderingly. It made sense; they hadn't been together for that long or been that conventional of a couple. They'd spent a lot of time together, alone, and if it wasn't for Jordan's habit of taking selfies when he thought he looked good, he wouldn't have even half this many.

"Neither did I. Then you went back to Chicago and it was all I had left." His voice dropped lower, almost confessional in tone. "I couldn't delete them, no matter how much I wanted to. One time, I almost got to that point, but I couldn't do it."

"Why not?" Reed asked.

Jordan chuckled. "I actually called Landon and he talked me out of it."

Reed couldn't help but smile at that. "So what you're telling me is that Landon is never going to let us live down the fact that he's at least partially responsible for getting us back together."

"Basically, yes."

"Come here," Reed said gruffly, and pulled Jordan into a tight embrace. "I love you. I never should have stopped telling you."

Jordan's words were muffled by the collar of Reed's shirt, but he still heard them loud and clear. "I love you too. I loved you from the moment you told me I needed a reservation."

The elevator dinged, informing Reed and Jordan that they had reached their destination—the *Five Points* floor, where, from the lights and music and noise, the annual Christmas party was definitely already underway.

"We're here, and all I already want is to go home," Reed sighed. It had been very hard after Jordan's gift to keep their hands to themselves and follow through with their plans to go to the party.

If Reed hadn't felt like he was duty-bound to apologize to Jemma for his terrible Secret Santa gifts, they probably wouldn't be here at all. They'd be back in bed, making up for too much lost time.

He told Jordan this as they stepped out of the elevator, and Reed was desperately in love but not too desperately in love to miss the guilty expression that flashed across his boyfriend's face.

Even a sixteen-month breakup couldn't make Reed forget what that expression meant. He'd known what it meant back in Chicago, and he definitely knew what it meant now, in LA. It meant Jordan had been spending too much time with Landon.

"Tell me," Reed said firmly.

"There might . . . um," Jordan hesitated. "Not technically, not *exactly,* be a Secret Santa exchange to apologize for."

Reed shot Jordan a look which he hoped was just as eloquent as the words he was being too nice to say. "What?"

"It might have been, sort of, kind of, a way for me to show you how much I love you still. Landon and I set it up so I'd get you and you'd get someone else." At least Jordan had the nerve to look ashamed.

"Oh my god," Reed said, throwing his hands up in the air. "And Jemma is a good friend of yours, which meant I had to talk to you to get ideas for what to get her."

Jordan made a face. "Yes . . . and no. I don't really know her all that well. She's Colin's best friend."

"Colin O'Connor was in on this!" Reed exclaimed. "Oh my god, I can't believe you. Why didn't you just text me, it would've been easier."

"Easier, but not better," Jordan retorted. "After so much time had passed, how could I possibly tell you I wanted you back without some big apology gesture?"

"That's it. You've definitely spent too much time with Landon." Reed didn't know how he felt about the deception; right now frustration was winning for being the most identifiable emotion he was feeling.

"You're mad," Jordan said softly, tugging him off to the side of the reception area. Thankfully they hadn't actually entered the party yet. "I get it. I shouldn't have lied to you, especially not after I promised never to do that again."

"I don't know if I am or not." Reed took a deep breath. "Was it even true when you said Quentin suggested me for the job? Or did Quentin think of me for the job because Landon thought of it first?" Reed wasn't mad, exactly, but he wanted answers. He wanted the truth.

"I don't know," Jordan said honestly. "All I know is that Nick came to me and said he wanted to hire you, if you were interested. He wanted to make sure I'd be okay with it."

Reed paced back and forth, clearly torn. "And you said yes."

"Of course I said yes!" Jordan said. "A chance to get us in the same physical location? A chance to be able to talk to you again? A chance to be able to really apologize, not just some lame apology text? I wasn't going to turn that down. Plus, you were perfect for the job."

"What if I didn't want to see you again? What if I didn't want to talk to you again?" Reed challenged. "What if I'd told you to go to hell?" Reed had almost done that; but in the end, he was endlessly grateful that he'd listened—both to Jordan, and to himself. Maybe Jordan's methods hadn't been completely aboveboard, but the feelings behind them had definitely been. Reed believed that completely.

"Then I would have left," Jordan admitted, and his voice was pained.

"You would have quit this job?" Reed knew he sounded extremely skeptical. "A job that you love?"

"There are other jobs. I'm lucky, I've made a decent amount of money, and I was smart with investments. I don't have to work," Jordan said.

"You would've just left me here, and what, chalked it up to a relationship gone bad?"

"I would have left and mourned you the rest of my fucking life, okay? Is that what you want to hear?" Jordan choked out, turning away so Reed wouldn't see the tears in his eyes.

"Yes," Reed exhaled. Jordan glanced up in surprise. "All I ever wanted was for you to tell me the truth about how you felt."

Jordan smiled, a little damp, but still so bright. Still one of the best things that Reed had ever seen.

"I told you I love you," he said softly. "I meant it then. I meant it half an hour ago. I'm going to mean it years from now."

"Good," Reed said. He believed him. He'd never believed anything more. "Now let's go home. We can get tacos anytime, and we shouldn't give Landon any more opportunities to be smug, don't you think?" He held out his hand and Jordan took it immediately. Gratefully.

"I won't mention that Landon might have won the pool then," Jordan said.

"Better not." Reed glanced over as he pressed the elevator button. "Please tell me you didn't bet against us."

"You're the best person I've ever met, I'd never dare," Jordan said, looking into Reed's eyes seriously.

Reed wanted to shake his head and laugh, because he loved his man, Slytherin traits and all.

"Do I want to ask what Landon won?" he asked instead, because Jordan already knew he loved him; the truth about how truly gone he was could stay hidden. For now, anyway. Maybe in the proposal that Reed knew he'd eventually make, he could tell Jordan that he loved him because he was a Slytherin, not in spite of it.

Jordan's smile was dazzling in the dim light of the elevator. "No. No, you do not."

The reason Reed knew he was so in love?

Because the idea of finding out exactly how Landon Patton has prepared to screw them over in the coming weeks actually looked like fun, if it meant he and Jordan were in it together.

Interested in more holiday offerings from Beth?

Coming November 18 is ***Merry Elf-ing Christmas***, a brand new whimsical holiday novel about an elf who doesn't belong in the North Pole and an engineer who doesn't know the thing that's missing from his life is magic.

Check out ***Fairytale of LaGuardia***, co-authored with A.E. Wasp, about a rookie hockey player and a washed up pitcher, who end up snowed in together during Christmas at the worst airport in the world.

INTERESTED IN READING MORE OF
BETH'S BOOKS?

CHECK OUT A FULL LIST OF TILES
BY SCANNING THE QR CODE
OR VISITING HER WEBSITE

WWW.BETHBOLDEN.COM/BOOKLIST

WANT TO FOLLOW BETH?

MAKE SURE YOU NEVER
MISS A RELEASE?

SCAN THE QR CODE BELOW
OR VISIT HER WEBSITE
FOR A SOCIAL MEDIA LIST,
NEWSLETTER SIGNUP,
AND SO MUCH MORE!

WWW.BETHBOLDEN.COM/ABOUT